DAVID
Is an Ugly Word

CINDY DORMINY

David Is an Ugly Word
Red Adept Publishing, LLC
104 Bugenfield Court
Garner, NC 27529
https://RedAdeptPublishing.com/

This is a work of fiction. Names, characters, places, and incidents either are the product of the author's imagination or are used fictitiously, and any resemblance to locales, events, business establishments, or actual persons—living or dead—is entirely coincidental.

To Maddie Rose. My favorite color is you.

Chapter 1

Michael lets out an exasperated groan when he notices the food on the kitchen table. As always, Monday has to be Chinese day. Michael and I may favor each other with our dark hair and eyes, but the similarities stop there. My twin just doesn't get it. The word *Chinese* has a pretty combination of blues, pinks, and greens. It's a perfect match for *Monday*.

"Kenzie, can't you think outside the crayon box for once?"

I arrange the to-go containers on the dining room table so the three of us can reach all the items, making sure the kung pao chicken is farthest away from me because the brown and gray next to the pink *N* is gross. "Nope. Monday is my night to choose the food, and I like Chinese."

He reaches for a fortune cookie, but I swat his hand away. "For once, I wish you would pick pizza."

On instinct, my nose scrunches up as I think about the word. It's such a gross-looking word. It shouldn't ruin a pleasant word like *Monday*. It matches better with *Friday*.

He opens the lo mein box and inhales the awesome aroma. His eyebrow quirks up. "Let me guess. This has something to do with your color system, right?"

Ever since I realized I see letters and numbers in color, I've been testing the significance of it. Now that I realize not all people have synesthesia, it must be a gift, and I have figured out ways it makes my life easier. It definitely helps me avoid ugly situations.

"Maybe," I say under my breath. "But don't say anything to Mom because she'll think it has something to do with the divorce, which by the way, is *not* going to happen."

My parents' pending divorce is another example of my "color thing" working in my favor. They will not get a divorce. It's obvious. Their colors match perfectly.

With his bare hand, Michael digs out a chunk of sesame chicken. Gross. "Sis, you have to admit it's been a whole lot quieter since Dad moved out."

I snort. "No, I won't, and your stupid band practicing in the garage makes it even worse."

He feigns shock. "We're going to be famous one day, and you'll wish you were nicer to the guys and more appreciative of our mix of grunge, blues, and indie rock."

"Blech. If I hear one more Nirvana song, I think my ears will bleed."

Michael gives me a one-shoulder shrug. "Yeah, that does get a bit much at times."

Mom walks into the kitchen with her phone cemented to her ear. I swear, ever since she's been dating Collin, she is worse than a teenager. She's on the phone all the time, and her sappy giggle makes me want to hurl.

Before Mom finishes her convo, I whisper to Michael, "Please don't mention my colors to her."

He rolls his eyes. "Whatever. It's just food."

"Thanks."

Mom finally has the decency to unhinge herself from her phone to inspect the meal. "Thanks for ordering, sweetie. Work has been so busy lately."

Work. Boyfriends. Divorce. Busy, busy, busy.

I paint on a fake smile and say, "No worries."

She scoops out some jasmine rice on to her plate and passes the box to Michael. "Another school year has begun. I cannot believe my babies are seniors."

Michael gives Mom the stink eye. "We aren't babies anymore."

She pinches his cheek. "You will always be my babies. Do you have any classes together?"

"Nope," Michael says. "And that's pretty good if you ask me."

"My schedule doesn't seem just right for some reason." I mull over Michael's choice of words: Pretty good, pretty. In my mind, I visualize my class schedule and finally realize why it hasn't felt right. I'm the biggest dummy on the planet. I know what I have to do. It's like a giant colorful light bulb went off in my head.

Small talk around the table drags out our meal, and I'm itching to run my idea past Michael. He'll think I'm bonkers, but I have to try. It's a brilliant plan.

Once we finish our meal and Mom is tucked away in her room, chatting with Collin, no doubt, Michael and I clean up the kitchen.

I clear my throat and say, "I was wondering if you would help me out with a teeny-tiny problem."

He sighs. "Did you get a virus on your computer again? Your personal IT expert is not always going to be around to clean up your messes."

I bump his hip with mine. "Surprisingly, it has nothing to do with technology. I need you to support me in something."

"What is it this time?"

"I was thinking about requesting a class schedule change."

He rinses a dish and hands it to me to dry. "Which class?"

"Er, all of them."

He chuckles. "Why?"

After I place the dish in the cabinet, I reach for the next one that he holds out. "Because they are not very..."

Michael freezes then smirks. "Let me guess. You don't want to take a class because the word has an ugly color."

I hold out my hands in defense. "Not exactly. I want to reorder my classes so they match with the days that have the same colors."

He gives me an "I just grew a third eye" expression. "What does that even mean, and why does it matter?"

"It's really hard to explain," I say, putting the dish away. "When colors match, they make me calmer. Somehow, pretty colors tend to give me guidance."

He hands me three forks. As I rinse them, he says, "You could just as easily use a Magic 8 Ball and get the same results. I think you're taking this whole color thing too far. Big deal, you can see letters and numbers in color. If you categorize food, and now classes, according to how pretty the words are, what's to stop you from doing the same with people?"

I cringe. "Actually..."

His eyes bug out of their sockets, then he points a finger at me. "David. That's why you hate David. Isn't it?"

With my eyes trained on the floor, I reply, "Maybe."

For a moment, he stares at the ceiling and, right when I think he's going to let it pass, he says, "Seriously? He's my best friend, and he used to be your best friend too."

"Can we get back to my class schedule situation?"

He starts to walk away, but I grab his arm. "I have an idea, and all I need you to do is go with me to Mrs. Tanner's office in the morning."

Michael shakes his head. "Why drag me into this?"

With a cheesy grin, I say, "Because she likes you. You are her number one fix-it dude."

Michael throws his hands in the air. "Whatever. Just don't mess with my schedule. I like it the way it is."

I tackle my twin in a big hug. "Oh, thank you so much. I promise everything will be fine."

He removes himself out of my grip and wags his head. "Just be careful what you wish for."

I stick my tongue out at him. Now that I've got Michael to support me, I have to see if my plan is feasible. Operation Synesthesia Schedule is up and running.

Chapter 2

Senior year. Yikes. While other kids at my school are doing campus tours, I sit at home, not knowing what's next for me. With no money, no colleges fighting over me, and no plan for my future, everything scares the crap out of me. I always thought I wanted to follow in Mom's footsteps and go to Bellevue University, but when she died, I didn't really care anymore. The only thing I have left of her is her old Mustang. Dad never could part with it, and I love it. It gets better with age. If it weren't for that old relic, I'd still be either taking the bus or bumming rides from my best friend and neighbor, Michael. I'm over at their house so much as it is, if I had to share a ride with him and his sister, Kenzie, aka my crush-that-will-never-be, she might spontaneously combust.

I push the Spaghetti-Os around on my plate while Dad and my little sister, Fiona, talk about the pros and cons of getting a dog. Fi may be a persistent eight-year-old, but I don't think she's ever going to win this fight.

"Dad, you rescue animals from bad homes. Don't you want us to help give one a good home?" She bats her pretty blue eyes for added effect. Mom always loved her little mini-me.

"Honey, if I took home every dog I recovered, we'd be up to our elbows in fur."

Fiona shrugs as she slurps down some of her dinner. "I don't see the problem."

I nudge Fiona with my shoulder. "I'll take you to the Humane Association so you can pet dogs all day long."

Dad holds up a hand to stop me. "Oh no, you don't. One look at those cute puppy dog eyes and she'll be begging you to adopt it." He points his spoon at me. "And we all know how you have no willpower when it comes to *her* puppy dog eyes."

Fiona grins. She knows I'm a pushover with her. Ever since Mom died when she was barely more than a toddler, I've gone a little overboard trying to be there for her. It's hard for Dad to provide for us and be around all the time. If I didn't think the world of her, it would be different, but I'd do anything for her. Except get a puppy without parental approval.

Dad gulps down the last of his tea then says, "Senior year. I can't believe it's here already."

I shake my head, and the long blond curls in my high fade cut fall in my eyes. "Me neither."

"Do you have a short list of colleges picked out?"

Short list. That's a term reserved for rich kids from a two-parent income family who can afford dozens of college applications and tours. My long and short lists consist of one college, and it's local. Even with in-state tuition, I'm not sure if Dad can foot the bill.

"I'm working on it."

The twinkle in his eyes fades as he says, "I'll do what I can, I promise. I do want you to have every chance to do what you love."

I shrug and hope he sees it as it's no big deal. "I can always play music even if I don't study it."

"Don't give up yet." Dad stacks our plates together and takes them to the sink. "But it never hurts to have a plan B just in case."

"And a plan C, D, and E wouldn't hurt either." I chuckle, hoping Dad and Fiona take it as a joke, but there's a hint of truth to it.

"How is band practice going?"

That's all it takes, and I'm back in my happy place again. "Getting better all the time. We're starting to really gel."

Dad glances over to Fiona, then in a hushed tone, he asks, "Is Kenzie still giving you the cold shoulder?"

Thanks, Pop. There goes my happy place. I don't know what I ever did to tick her off, but the last few years have been rough. I went from being her best friend to public enemy number one almost overnight.

I bring our tea glasses to the kitchen and dump the remaining ice into the sink. "Yep. At least we don't have any classes together, so I don't have to see her sneering at me all day long."

"I miss Kenzie," Fiona says, handing Dad the leftovers. I was hoping she didn't overhear this conversation because it's better if she stays out of it. As hard as it was when Kenzie went cold on me, it was triply difficult on my little sister. She worshiped the ground Kenzie walked on, and to see that go away for my sister was very painful.

"Friends grow apart sometimes," Dad says.

Trying to sound more upbeat than I feel, I say, "It's okay. The band is all I need right now."

Dad pops me with the dishtowel and says, "You never know what tomorrow might bring."

"Sure I do. It will bring Tuesday."

Fiona boos me, but Dad sees an opening and he takes it.

"Did you hear about the restaurant on the moon? The food is great, but there's no atmosphere."

Fiona groans. "Dad, that was an especially bad joke."

He rocks back on his heels. "I'm the best at bad dad jokes."

"No argument there," I say as I make my way to my bedroom.

Maybe Dad is right. This could be my year. I could have a great senior year with my band buds, find a college I can afford to go to, and study music. Maybe even Kenzie will look my way again. I never know what tomorrow will bring, but I'm not going to hold my breath, especially when it comes to her. She's made it clear she hates me, and if I avoid her, all will be fine.

Chapter 3

After spending the better part of the night researching course offerings, I finally found the perfect schedule. But if Mrs. Tanner doesn't rearrange my classes, it will have all been for nothing. It has to be perfect, and if my rationale doesn't do the trick, her favorite cookies I whipped up in the middle of the night will. And to seal the deal, I'm bringing Michael along while I plead my case. No teacher in this school can resist my twin brother's charm, or his ability to fix any computer problem, so my plan is as good as done.

As all the other kids rush out of school like the building is on fire, heading to part-time jobs or to hang out at the Donut Den, I drag Michael through the hallway toward the guidance counselor's office. I clutch my Rubbermaid container that is a few cookies shy of being full. Michael insisted on an edible payment for his forced participation. Of course, I had to sample a few as well, but those don't count. Quality control is important.

"She's never going to go for it."

I give Mike the side-eye as we head toward the front of the school. "Of course she will. I have a plan."

Mike groans. "Shocker. You always have a plan. The guys are coming over to practice our new song, so let's make this fast."

He doesn't deserve an eye roll. That stupid band rattling the windows of our house day after day gets on my last nerve. Michael needs a new hobby, and it wouldn't hurt any if he got a new best friend too.

"I've got it all figured out and have thought about every roadblock she could possibly throw my way."

Michael chuckles. "It's completely possible she will flat out say no. I bet she wants to go home too, so don't expect she'll want to sit here all night long debating with you."

He has a point.

At Mrs. Tanner's door, I pull back and take a deep, cleansing breath. "I need this."

He chews on the side of his mouth, the telltale sign he's mulling over my plea and about to give in. After an exasperated huff, he nudges me toward the guidance counselor's door. "I can't believe you dragged me into this."

I squeeze his shoulders. "You're the best brother ever."

"I get that a lot. Just leave my schedule alone. You hear me?"

I salute my older-by-three-minutes brother. "Yes sir." After another large exhale, I knock on the door.

"Enter."

Michael opens the door and motions with his head for me to go first. Mrs. Tanner's scrunched-up face doesn't give me much confidence she's in a good mood. When her eyes flick up and land on Michael, her expression takes a one-eighty turn. She waves him over.

"Ah, Mr. Hamilton, just the person I need to see. I've done it again. I can't find the file."

She stands to let my brother sit at her desk. While he clicks around on her computer, she nibbles on a fingernail. Clutching the container of cookies, I slink down into a chair on the other side of her desk, then pull out a sheet of paper from my book bag while he goes into full geek mode.

In about three seconds and a dozen clicks, he smiles up at her. "There's your document. I made a shortcut on your desktop to make it easier to find."

She sighs and raises her hands in celebration. "Hallelujah. You are a-maze-balls."

I hate it when she tries to act cool, but now that she's in a good mood, it's time to pounce.

"Mrs. Tanner, I was wondering if it would be possible to switch my schedule around a tiny bit."

She shakes her head as she reclaims her desk chair. "Why would you want your schedule changed?"

"I'm glad you asked." Michael settles into the chair next to me as I place the sheet of paper on her desk. I made a chart that includes my current, ugly schedule and an alternative one that is much better and way prettier.

She slides the paper closer to her with one finger, taps it a few times before she shakes her head. "I don't think so. Most classes are filled."

"But—"

"Do you need a more challenging selection?"

"No. It's just that..." I glance down at my hands as they form tight balls on the top of the cookie container.

Michael clears his throat. "My sister only wants to switch the order of her classes. You see, she's a morning person." He peeks over to me. "Right?"

"Yes, and none of the classes I want to switch into are full. I checked before I even came to you."

There goes her crinkled brow again. She turns to her computer and taps the keyboard as she mumbles something under her breath. Nothing happens.

Michael leans over her desk and points to her right hand. "I think you have the caps lock button turned on."

"Oh." She bounces in her chair like a fifteen-year-old hearing the latest hit from PRETTYMUCH. She does a tappity-tap on the keyboard as I peek over to Michael. Twinstinct tells me he's hoping this works out for me, no matter how ridiculous it sounds. She sighs. "I don't normally do these kinds of things because, you know, if I do for one, I have to do for all."

Please not the singsong voice.

My heart sinks. I know if I don't get my schedule changed, I won't be able to concentrate and my grades will tank. No one understands that.

Michael turns to me and winks. "Mrs. Tanner, if you still want me to defrag your hard drive, I think I'll have some time next week."

I almost choke on my saliva at how dirty that sounds, but knowing him, I'm sure it's only a geeky term.

Her eyes light up. "Would it make my outdated machine run faster?"

He shrugs. "It can't hurt."

She stares from me to Michael then back to her computer screen. "Uh-oh. We have a problem. You can't change to that particular class for first period because Michael is in that class also. We prefer to keep siblings in separate classes."

Well, fudge. "Yeah, but it's only independent study."

Mrs. Tanner cringes. "I don't know."

Michael nudges me and motions to my lap where the cookie container rests.

"Oh, I almost forgot." I place the plastic container on her desk and pop open the lid. "I made these for you."

When the chocolate-and-oatmeal aroma wafts over to Mrs. Tanner, her eyes roll back into her head while she grabs for a cookie. She stuffs one in her mouth and grips the edge of her desk to let out a satisfied moan.

"Yum. These are so good. How did you know these were my favorite?"

"Must be my lucky day." *Liar.*

With one more big swallow, she scans her computer screen again. After a few taps on the keys, she prints out a document and hands it to me. "Our little secret."

My jaw drops. "Really?"

She nods. "If you tell anyone I can be bribed with cookies, I will switch you back. Do you understand?"

Happy dance time. "Yes, ma'am."

She points toward the door. "I don't want to see you anymore for the rest of the semester."

Fireworks explode in my brain. I wanted this to happen, but I never fully believed it would. I could kiss her now if I didn't think it was inappropriate.

"You'll never see me again."

She checks her watch and huffs. "Now, I'm going to be late for my Zumba class."

The image of her in workout gear sends a shiver down my spine.

We stand to leave, and right as we get to her door, she clears her throat. "Michael, don't forget about defragging my computer."

He pins me in my place with a stare, and I know I'm going to pay severely for his involvement in my plan later on. "Yes, ma'am."

Mrs. Tanner shoos us out of her office, and as soon as I close the door behind us, I inhale my first breath in five minutes. Relief washes over me as I float down the hallway and dance around Michael, but all he does is roll his eyes.

"You are the strangest person I know."

I point my finger at him. "Our DNA is almost the same, so that means you are strange too."

He shakes his head. "No one is odder than you."

I shrug as I beam with pride that my plan worked. Even though I put a lot of thought into my request to minimize rejection, I still had a hint of doubt she'd go for it. But now, I am sure this semester is going to be epic.

As he unlocks his truck, he laughs again. "You think you have it all figured out with this color stuff, don't you?"

"Yep. Like I said, my colors never let me down."

"Be careful what you wish for."

Pfft. Michael isn't going to steal my joy. This is the best day ever, and tomorrow will be the beginning of the perfect semester. It's going to be beautiful.

Chapter 4

Propping my feet up on the porch rail, I review the lyrics to my latest song. Some days, I stare at a blank page for hours, and then other days, like today, the words flow out of me like a deep blue river. I can't make my hands move fast enough to write down my ideas. I know I only have a few more minutes before the band begins congregating in Hamilton's garage for practice, so I need to get this one last line down. It's so close to being perfect.

I chug a glass of iced tea as I play a loop of words over and over in my mind. Nothing seems to match exactly what I'm trying to convey. Just as the exact word is on the tip of my tongue, Hamilton's Ford F150 pickup truck rambles down the road, radio blaring. When he gets to my house, he toots the horn and waves. From the passenger seat, Kenzie's head turns in my direction, a scowl consuming her face. Michael and Kenzie are so much alike, except she is way better looking in shorts. So much better.

As he parks his truck in their driveway across the street, I return the wave. "Hamilton, I'll see you in an hour."

"Sounds good."

Kenzie, with her head held high, takes the stairs to their front porch two at a time with more bounce in her step than she's had in years. Usually, the most common word I would use to describe her would have to be crabby. But today, she acts peppy. I do a synonym search and find the perfect word for my song: Zestful. *Thanks, Kenz.* Even though she would be furious if a word that describes her to a T made it into my song, she never has to know. It will be my little secret. Besides, I don't need the wrath of Mackenzie Hamilton bearing down on me. I'll never know what I did to make her so annoyed at me. I stopped trying to figure out her brain a long time ago.

I stand to stretch out my stiff muscles before I head back into my house. Fiona reclines on the couch, eating Pringles while she watches an episode of *Prince Not So Charming*. She's watched all five seasons so many times I wonder if Prince Gus Walker lives here. And I've caught myself on more than one occasion chanting, "Keep calm and put your crown on." I can't wait until she moves on to another heartthrob.

"Hey, kiddo. Will Catarina ever figure out Gus is a royal?"

Fiona rolls her eyes in a perfect preteen fashion. "Don't you have college applications to work on?"

"Shut up," I say with a snarl on my face as I ramble down the hallway toward my bedroom. She is a teenager in an eight-year-old body.

From the living room, she yells, "Are you feeling peckish? Tee-hee."

Little sisters. What's worse than having one is admitting they are right, especially when they know it. Bellevue University is the perfect college for me, but I know Dad can't afford it. He's still fighting off bill collectors years after Mom's death. I guess part of me doesn't want to apply because if I do get accepted, Dad will have a disappointed face when he can't give me what I want. What I really need is a big, fat scholarship.

I open my five-year-old, second-hand laptop—*Thanks, Hamilton*—and pull up the website I know by heart. Filling out the application is pretty basic: name, address, blah, blah, blah. My ACT scores are solid, and my GPA is above the minimum requirements, so I am off to a good start.

A knock on my bedroom door scares me so bad I bang my knee on the edge of my desk. Dad chuckles as he enters my room, his blond hair a mess as usual after a long day being an animal resource officer. Usually, he comes home smelling like dog crap, but today, he looks like he rolled in mud.

"What happened to you?"

He leans against the door frame and groans. "I had to rescue ten puppies that were stuck under this dilapidated house. The pipes had been leaking for months, and it was either me crawling under there in the muck or Gretta. And you know..."

I let out a snort. Gretta is a wonderful person and has done more than her fair share to ensure Fiona and I had some motherly love, but she's about sixty and as big around as she is tall. If she went under the house, Dad would have to rescue puppies and a rotund lady too.

"Did you save all the puppies?"

Dad peeks down the hall toward Fiona before he continues in a hushed tone. "Yeah, and as soon as they are up for adoption, I'm going to get one for Fi."

The grin on my face hurts my cheeks. Fiona has wanted a pup ever since Mom died, and Dad's put it off because he can barely afford to feed two kids, let alone a furball too.

"Dad, she's going to squeal for days."

He grins. "She deserves it." His smile fades, and I know he's thinking about Mom. "I wish I could do more for you kids."

I shrug, hoping I seem like it's no big deal, but it is.

He points to my laptop screen. "That's a good school."

"Yeah, but kind of pricey."

He nods. "They all are. But you can apply for financial aid. I'm sure we'll qualify." He points to my screen again. "Check out what's under the 'scholarship opportunities.' You never know. Leave no stone unturned. I want you to go there if that's the one for you."

"I will. And it is."

Dad glances down at his muddy clothes. "I better take a shower before dinner. Do you have band practice tonight?"

"Yep. I wrote another song too."

He pops me on the back. "You're so talented."

What he lacks in funds, he makes up for in support and love. If I had to go through life with only one parent, I'm so glad I'm stuck with him. "Thanks, Dad."

When he leaves, my eyes find their way back to the scholarship link. It can't hurt to look. Most are for minority students or those with diverse backgrounds. Another on the list is titled "Full Scholarship—Awarded to One Student Per Year." My heart does a flip-flop in my chest as my mouse hovers over the link. Maybe I have what it takes to get a full ride. This could be my answer.

Out loud, I read the description. "The Bellevue University School of Music and Music Business awards one outstanding student the Henry Williams scholarship. This is a full scholarship, and candidates must have the minimum requirements to be admitted to the university."

I lick my lips and rub the palms of my hands together. So far, so good. "A deep desire to perform as well as write music that is unique, creative, and personal." I sit up straighter.

Hello, Bellevue. Here I come. This is me.

"Secondly, the ideal candidate will have experience performing in front of an audience and incorporating original music and lyrics."

I cringe. Our band is getting there, but at least we have performed at a few parties. No one has to know they were for my little sister's friends.

"And lastly, Bellevue University believes in recruiting well-rounded individuals. The ideal candidate must not only be musically and lyrically talented, they must provide evidence of their marketing ability in regard to self-promotion."

Well, crud. I'm not liking this at all. I swallow hard as I read the last and most damaging statement of all. "Students interested in this scholarship should submit a link to their professional website. Sections should include at least, but not limited to the following: a main 'about' page, tour dates, merchandise, and especially a blog."

My heart sinks into my feet. I don't know how to do any of that stuff. I'm an artist, a musician, a songwriter, not a freaking web expert. I close my laptop and flop down on my bed, making it creak under my weight. My forearm rests over my head to block the light from my eyes. I want to crawl into a dark cave and never come out. This is the beginning of the worst semester ever.

Chapter 5

Thanks to Mrs. Tanner, every class is now in the perfect order. All is right with the world. It's all pretty again, and a bonus is now I have first period with the best person I could imagine sharing a womb with.

I plop into the desk beside my brother and give Michael a thumbs-up. He shakes his head. No matter how I try to explain it, he still thinks I'm weird. I'm calmer when numbers and letters match up and align with their appropriate colors. It may be a tad bit odd, but my colors let me know who to trust. They never fail me.

Michael lets out a chuckle. "I cannot believe you bribed her with her favorite cookies so you could have first-period independent study."

I clap my hands, unable to control my satisfaction. "And second period is now science."

He leans over his desk to whisper, "Let me guess. English is third period now because the E and the three..."

I nod. "Yep. Same color. I have balance."

He pinches the bridge of his nose. I hate it when he does that. It's such a dad thing to do. "I'm sure it's those three minutes you had all by your lonesome in the uterus that messed you up."

I give him a smirk and pull out a notebook. "My system works. Don't knock it. I bet you could see the colors, too, if you tried."

"Yeah, yeah. Are you sure the real reason you want in this class isn't so you can gawk at Eli?" He bats his eyes in a pathetic impersonation of a girl.

Even so, heat rises on my neck at the mention of the cutest boy in school. "That is a side benefit. One that I'm not going to complain about."

"Well, you still owe me. And thanks to you, I now have to fix Mrs. Tanner's computer."

The snort leaves my throat before I can stop it. "Sorry about that. And don't even tell me what 'defrag' means."

"It's not as dirty as it sounds."

I stare at my geeky twin. "Sounds exhilarating."

When Eli strolls into the room, I feel my cheeks flame. His jet-black hair in a flat top is too cool for words. But when he scoots down the aisle to take the very back seat on the far side of the room, my grin fades. Darn it. Now, I only get to gawk when he enters and exits instead of when I'm pretending to study the entire class period.

"Phooey."

Michael glances around the room. "Yeah, sorry about that. I guess I should have told you he likes to sit in the back of the room so no one sees how stoned he is."

"But he's so..." I actually let out a pathetic sigh.

"Pretty?"

I rest my chin in my hand and sigh again. "Exactly. The E and the L match so well."

Michael motions with his head. "Unlike him?"

I peel my eyes away from the perfection sitting in the back of the room to the king of uglies. David leans against the door frame with a huge, surprised grin on his face.

As David saunters into the room, never breaking eye contact with me, I lean over to Michael and whisper, "You didn't tell me *he* was in this class."

Michael fist bumps David. "You didn't ask."

"What's up, Hamilton? Hey, Mackenzie. Fancy seeing you here."

I fumble with my backpack to retrieve a notebook. "Don't call me that, David Shaw." Just saying his name out loud gives me a fit of nausea.

When I think things couldn't get worse, he has the nerve to sit in the desk right in front of me. Ugh. This is not going as planned.

Girls all over the school talk about how hot he is and how they would donate a kidney to run their hands through his wavy blond hair, but I don't understand the attraction. All that goes through my brain when I think of him is a muddled mess of browns mixed with gray-blues. His colors are so awful, and I have to see his ugly mug more than I care to since he lives across the street. Not to mention, he practically lives at our house.

At least three girls let out a collective exhale of delight when he leans over to tie his shoe, exposing his back and the waistband of his boxer briefs. *Oh, please. That's the oldest trick in the book.* He's not worth getting worked up over, especially since David is an ugly word.

Mollie, my best friend in the whole wide world, scoots into the room a nanosecond before Mr. Carter shuts the door with his foot. Yay! We have a class together.

In one hand, Mr. Carter carries a monster-sized coffee mug with the inscription, "After Monday and Tuesday, even the calendar says WTF." In the other hand, he balances a stack of papers. He clears his throat super loud, I guess to get our attention. Mollie slides into the seat on the other side of Michael and waves at me as she piles her auburn hair on top of her head and secures it into a bun with a pencil. Mr. Carter plunks the mug down on his desk and proceeds to pass out the packets of papers.

"Take one and pass the rest back but place it facedown on your desk. Mackenzie, I was notified yesterday afternoon you'd be joining us. Nice to have you in this class. You actually did me a favor. Now, about the project I briefly mentioned yesterday."

A chorus of groans bellow through the room.

"Thanks a lot, Kenzie," Eli says.

I snap my head around to find him shooting me daggers with his eyes. I take back everything I said about his cuteness because his insides don't match his exterior. Ignoring the jab, I huff as I cross my arms and return my attention to the front of the class.

"What I meant was she made the class size an even number, which will make the situation ideal." After everyone has a packet, he turns on his laptop and projector. He sits on the edge of the desk and takes a gulp of coffee. "I know most independent studies are a way to catch up on other homework or get a nap, but we are going to do a social experiment."

More groans, but this sounds like fun to me.

He waves off the naysayers. "For the next two weeks, you will be... married, for lack of a better word, to another classmate."

Gasp.

He clicks the mouse on his laptop. "Turn your papers over."

The rustle of papers overpowers the protests, then Harper, the most annoying girl in the entire world, squeals.

Mr. Carter rolls his eyes. "You and your spouse will make decisions together, learn what the other wants in a partner, work on a budget, ya-da, yada, yada. At the end of the project, you and your partner will present your outcomes and what you learned from the experiment."

The usual friend groups begin to talk about the project as Mr. Carter continues. "Before you start pairing up, I've randomly assigned you each a partner for this project to break up the usual cliques."

Charlie, another member of Michael's band, lets out the F word on that one. If he gets paired up with Harper, he'll be whipped into submission before the day is over. And if I get paired with Eli after he made that comment, things could get awkward superfast. Under my desk, I cross my fingers that I get paired with Michael. I would rather have a fake relationship with my brother than I would with most people in this room. We practically share a brain anyway.

I glance at Michael, and the twinstinct kicks in. He winks, knowing exactly what I'm thinking.

Mr. Carter clicks a button on his laptop and displays a spreadsheet onto the projector screen so we can see the pairings easier. He scrunches his brow for the slightest second. "Huh. Oh well."

Several "woo-hoos" fly across the room, and more than a few "ughs" erupt. I'm too afraid to look. David lays his head on his desk in a fit of laughter. Whatever. Michael nudges me, and since I have to find out eventually, I force myself to glance at the screen.

This can't be happening. My lungs won't expand to let in any air. This is an epic fail.

"No, no, no."

Michael leans over to whisper in my ear, "Oh yes, yes, yes." He pats my back as if that's going to stop my panic attack.

"I'm paired with…" I can't even say it out loud.

David rotates his wide shoulders around until we are face-to-face. With a grin big enough to show his molars, he says, "Well, hello there, wifey poo."

I should have left my schedule the way it was. This is getting very ugly really fast.

Chapter 6

Hamilton and I watch Kenzie plead with Mr. Carter over our group pairing. Never in a million years did I think this would happen. For once, we'll have to be in the same room and carry on a conversation without her running away like she's going to throw up. Her panicked state makes it clear how she feels about me. It's not worth figuring out, but I'm going to take this opportunity. Before the project is over, we'll be friends again. Maybe more.

Don't jump that far ahead.

I don't care if it's required time together. We'll be forced to share the same air. Maybe we can get past whatever it is that makes her hate me. From the first day they moved into the house across the street in our boring little neighborhood with cookie-cutter, one-story ranch homes, I knew she was the one for me. When I met her brother, it was obvious we would be friends for life, but when he dragged his twin sister over to meet me, I couldn't form words. For the longest time, we were all friends—until we weren't anymore.

It seems like only yesterday, except somewhere along the way, we went from being known as the three twins, to the Hamilton and D show: wherever he was, so was I. Somewhere along the way, Kenzie turned on me for some reason. Even Michael doesn't understand it, or at least, that's what he tells me. That twinstinct, as Michael calls it, is pretty powerful, stronger than a friendship, so he may know more than he lets on and is sworn to secrecy.

Hamilton understands how it kills me to be in their house, sleeping over under the same roof with her totally ignoring me. He made it crystal clear that no matter how she feels about me, we are still buds and she has to get over it. I am always welcome in the Hamilton house. Even their mother made me an honorary member of their family. And after today's turn of events... let's just say I've never been so happy to work on a school project in my life.

Hamilton pats me on the back, knocking me out of my thoughts. "You think Carter's going to give in and let her switch partners?"

I shrug as I watch our teacher shake his head for the tenth time. "Doesn't look like it."

Kenzie flails her hands all over the place, making animated gestures as Carter stares at the ceiling, apparently trying to convey to her the conversation is over. She glances over at me then gives me the sneer of a lifetime. This isn't my fault, but I know I'm going to pay for it with my sanity.

"What if she refuses to work with me?"

Hamilton chews on a pen cap as we watch Kenzie plead her case. "I don't think she has a choice, bro. They already rearranged her entire schedule to make her happy. She needs to live with this."

Kenzie folds her arms over her chest and lets out a big huff.

"Yeah, what's up with that?"

Michael chuckles. "You know how Kenzie is. She gives weird a bad name."

Weird and adorable. But mostly weird.

"But it looks like you will be the beneficiary of her choices. It could be what gets the ice queen off her throne with you."

God, I hope so, but I have more important things to think about. "What do you know about web design?"

Hamilton's eyes light up. "You mean HTML?"

"Huh?"

"You know, hypertext—"

I hold up a hand to stop his computer science babble. "I mean, do you know how to design a kick-ass website?"

He shakes his head. "I know the programming part, but I couldn't design anything to save my life."

Well, crap. He's the only one who comes to mind for me to ask. "Do you know anyone who would want to help me with a band website?"

"No, but if I think of someone, I'll let you know."

Carter points to me, and Kenzie stomps a foot before she marches back to her desk.

"Hurricane Kenzie dead ahead." Under his breath, Hamilton adds, "Just nod and smile. It's easier that way."

Her hand brushes my arm as she passes me. She then slumps back into her chair with a huge groan.

"Kenzie, I—"

She holds up a hand to stop me from saying another word. "Don't." She trains her eyes on the packet for our project. I count at least three groans before she moves past the first page.

Mr. Carter clicks the keyboard on his laptop again and reveals the list of contents for the project. "Sorry for the delay. Where were we? Oh, yes, some of these exercises are meant to be done together, and some can be completed alone, but I expect you to review with your partner and discuss *everything*." He pins Kenzie in her seat with his stare before he continues. "I use the term 'partner' because we have one male-male pairing."

Eli and Charlie fist bump, so I assume they're cool with it.

Kenzie huffs. "Seriously? You set them up as a couple? You know they aren't gay, right?"

Mr. Carter shrugs. "Random pairings. It could have been any two guys or girls, but remember, none of this is real, and they don't seem to mind."

Charlie pinches Eli's cheek, which makes me feel like I entered the Twilight Zone. Charlie is the geekiest guy on the planet, but he's cool, and Eli is the big man on campus.

Eli says, "I don't mind. I'd rather be paired with this dude than any chick in the class. Too much drama."

A collective gasp as well as multiple high fives fill the room.

Hamilton laughs until Mollie catches his attention. His grin fades when he realizes his partner isn't happy with him. He clears his throat. "Except for you, my honey pie for the next few weeks."

Mollie's face turns as red as her hair. This should be interesting. Everyone except for Hamilton knows how bad she has it for him. He's so clueless, but he has a secret crush on her, too, so this pairing could be exactly what they need to get past their shyness.

"Mollie, don't you want to trade with me?" Kenzie begs with her eyes. I think she would get on her knees if she could.

Mollie shakes her head. "Can't do that. It's against rule number one. No partner swaps. And why would you want to be married to your brother?" She crinkles her freckled nose. "Ew."

The class giggles. I rotate my body so I can get a better view of Kenzie's perspiration-covered face.

She closes her eyes and mumbles something, then takes a deep breath. When our eyes meet, she has determination written all over her face. "We better get a good grade."

I lean over so my mouth is next to her ear, causing her peach shampoo scent to waft into my nose. "I promise we will make an A."

She blinks before she bites her lip.

Mr. Carter taps his laptop again. "Okay, listen up. In the back of the packet, you will see the rubric for how you will be graded. This does count toward your senior project hours, so take it seriously. You might learn something about yourself. Take the next fifteen minutes to complete the first worksheet with your partner, the 'are you right for each other' form."

Desks scuff on the floor while the class scoots around to get closer to their fake spouses. Kenzie and I stare at one another. Chatter surrounds us, and I wait for Kenzie to say something, anything. She swallows. I flip the page to get to the assigned worksheet.

"First question: Do I sometimes eat in bed?"

"Nope. Never." She scribbles on her page. Nope. She *never* does that except for every time I've passed by her room on the way to Hamilton's. She typically sprawls across her bed, a book in one hand and a bag of baked chips in the other. Yeah, sure, she *never* eats in bed.

She reads the next question. "Do you prefer shopping at bargain stores or small but classy shops? I like the classy ones." She sits straighter in her chair as she circles her answer.

I snort and look down at her Birkenstocks, the ones she bought at the Southern Thrift Store last summer and bragged about her great one-dollar purchase. I peek back at her and quirk an eyebrow. As if she can read my mind, she scoots her feet farther under her desk so I can't see her lie-confirming secondhand shoes.

"Okay. Next one. When it comes to television, would you rather watch a game show, a reality show, or an old movie?" This should be good. I know for a fact she can't stand reality shows, and no matter how many times she's seen her favorite movie, *The Princess Bride*, she'll stop what she's doing to watch it again.

She shrugs. "Easy. Game shows."

I cover her small hand with mine, making her stop circling the answer. "Kenz, don't sabotage this project by lying."

She snatches her hand from underneath mine like it electrocuted her then crosses her arms over her chest. "I don't know what you mean."

I scoot my desk chair closer to hers, so close my shoulder brushes hers, causing her to shiver. "You forget we've been neighbors since grade school, and I've lived half my life at your house."

"Don't remind me."

"Most of that time, I... I thought we were friends."

She chews on her bottom lip as she stares at her paper.

I lower my voice to make sure no one overhears us. "I don't know what I did to make you despise me, but please, I need a good grade on this. It would mean a lot to me if you would try to work with me instead of against me. You can go back to hating me when this is over."

Her jaw drops, and suddenly, I don't notice anyone else in the room. It's as if we are the only two people around. The chatter from the class fades away, and all that's left is me and Kenz gaping at one another.

She swallows hard as if there is a wad of crud stuck in her throat. "I don't hate you. I..." She peers down at her paper. "I can't explain it."

I wave her off. "It doesn't matter."

She takes a deep breath. "You're right. It's a class project. It's not like we're a real couple or anything like that." Kenzie lets out a nervous chuckle.

My heart sinks. I've been crushing on her ever since I was twelve years old, the day she held me while I bawled like a baby. It was the night my mother passed away. In my eyes, she's always been my girl, no matter if she doesn't feel the same way.

Kenzie scans the room. "Harper and Tiffany are not happy we're paired together."

I peek over my shoulder. Tiffany, my one attempt at a girlfriend, throws daggers at me with her eyes. She's by far the prettiest girl in the class on the outside, but she is pure meanness on the inside. Been there, done that. Got the "I dated Harper, and all I got was a knife in the back" T-shirt.

"I think I would beg my dad to be homeschooled if I got paired with her."

Kenzie giggles. God, I love her laugh. It sends a mushy, bubbly sensation through my insides. "Why didn't I think of that? I could be homeschooled."

I point a finger at her. "Too late now, *Mrs. Shaw.*"

She shakes her head and does her best not to smile by pressing her lips into a thin line. "Oh no, Mr. Shaw. I am a woman of the twenty-first century. I'll keep my maiden name, thank you very much."

My mouth splits open in a wide grin. At least we're off to a decent start. If I can keep this up, I may survive this project with my balls intact.

Mr. Carter claps his hands. "Before you leave, make sure you straighten up the desks. Tonight, work on the 'how do you see each other' form on your own, and together, complete the 'how compatible are you' questionnaire."

Grumbles erupt throughout the room.

He snaps his fingers. "Oh and, guys, tomorrow, bring a ring or something to signify your union. We'll have our ceremonies in class."

Even louder groans fill the room. Kenzie adjusts her desk so it's back in line with the others then scoops up her book bag. "I hope you don't have to buy too many gumballs before you get my ring out of the machine."

I chuckle as I watch her retreating form walk out of the room. I won't need a gumball machine to get her ring. I already have it.

Chapter 7

In silence, Michael drives us home in his beat-up truck. He knows better than to bring up today's events. What started as the best day ever turned into a train wreck before first period was over. Thank goodness the rest of my day was uneventful.

When I can't stand the silence anymore, I ask, "So, you and Mollie, huh?" I glance over to catch Michael's mouth twitch.

His face turns an adorable shade of pink. "Yeah. I dodged a bullet on that one. Tiffany would have neutered me before our wedding night."

The thought of my brother marrying that she-devil, even on a temporary, fake basis, sends shivers down my spine. "Tif's a piece of work. I think she'll have a run for her money with Rhett." I snort at the thought of those two egos in one household. "No one loves Rhett more than Rhett."

"So true." He turns into our boring, bland neighborhood and begins the trek to the end of the long road toward our house. "The pairings are pretty interesting, don't you think?"

"Ugh. Mine is the worst."

He gives me a playful shove on the shoulder. "Be nice. David is a good guy. Your project will be a no-brainer for both of you. You know so much about each other already."

"You are correct. Since we have nothing to learn, my project's done." I love my logic.

He flicks my nose with his index finger. "Maybe it's not David you need to learn something about. You could need to learn some things about yourself."

I blink at him like an idiot. "You suck."

Michael cackles as he pulls into our driveway and throws his truck into park. "Think of it this way. This will be a scientific experiment to justify your 'color theory' of people's names."

I hate it when he uses air quotes. It's such a chick thing to do, but he does have a point. Ever since I confessed to him how I see letters and numbers as colors, he's given me grief. This could be exactly what I need to validate how accurate my color system is. David's letters are really, really ugly, and ugly names always let me down. Michael's name is pretty, and he's never failed me. Mollie is the same way. And as soon as Mom and Dad realize their colors complement each other, things will be perfect at home because they are meant to be together, not living apart.

Once I realized how my synesthesia helps me categorize people into good and bad, life became so much easier. Now, I don't have to go through the heartbreak when someone lets me down. I know from the get-go how they will behave, so I don't have to rely on guesswork anymore. However, that only works when I have complete control over the situation. I'm stuck doing this stupid project with David, an ugly name, so I am out of control on this one, and that makes my insides twitch.

But Michael is right. All I have to do is endure a few weeks with David at my side all the time, and I'll prove it to Michael once and for all: ugly names equate to ugly outcomes.

There is one tiny wrinkle in my method. David doesn't know anything about my synesthesia or why I avoid him. He never understood why almost overnight I went from hanging out with him all the time to ignoring him. Every time he sees me, his eyes plead for me to acknowledge him like he's hoping this will be the day I get over myself. It's not that simple.

By the doe-eyed expression he gets when I walk into a room, I know he has a huge crush on me, and this project will be the perfect way to show him we are not compatible. Maybe once and for all, David will figure out we are not meant to be a couple, then he can stop pining for me, trying his best to win back my favor. God, I sound like someone from the olden days, like when my parents were young. David and I will never date. We can't even be friends. It's not going to happen, and this experiment will show it without me being the bad guy.

"Is Mollie coming over to work on your project?"

Michael follows me up the sidewalk toward our front door. "Yep. Five o'clock."

The rumble of David's old Mustang rolling into his driveway across the street catches our attention. He crawls out of the car and flings his book bag over his shoulder. I know the moment he sees us by the way he freezes.

When Michael closes the door behind us, I ask him, "Is he coming this way?"

"He always comes over here. We have the good junk food."

I make a beeline down the hallway to my bedroom and close the door behind me just in time to hear the front door squeak open and David's deep voice rumbling through the house. Dropping my book bag to the floor, I fling off my shoes and collapse onto my bed. I try to focus on my Pink Floyd poster, but even that doesn't give me any ideas on how to get through the next couple of weeks without wanting to pinch someone's head off. On autopilot, my gaze lands on my big picture window, which is directly across the street from David's window. His house is a mirror image of ours. Many nights, when we were little, Michael and I would sneak out of our house through my window to avoid the creaky front door, tiptoe across the street, and climb through David's window. It was the perfect way to enjoy hot summer nights without parental supervision. His father worked crazy hours, so he never caught us, and my parents thought we were safely tucked away in our bedrooms. It was fun before it got unfun.

A knock on my door makes me jump. Knowing exactly who it is, I say, "Kenzie's not home."

David chuckles and opens the door anyway. Typical. He clenches a paper bag with his teeth as he hugs a gallon jug of milk under one arm while carrying two glasses with the other. With his foot, he kicks the door closed behind him. He drops the bag onto my stomach.

"Oof."

"I thought we might get hungry working on the packet. Married life is tough stuff."

I fish a cookie from the bag and chomp down on it. "So very thoughtful of you to bring cookies that *I* baked from *my* kitchen."

He snatches the cookie out of my hand and eats the rest.

"Hey."

"I brought the milk. That has to count for something." He pours two glasses of milk and hands one to me before settling down on the floor in front of my bed.

I take a swig from my glass. "I guess the sooner we start on this project, the sooner we can be done."

David bites into a cookie, leaving crumbs on his scruffy chin. "Now, now. We aren't going to be done for a long time."

"Don't remind me."

He stands, grabs the bag of cookies with one hand, and takes me by the other, making me squeak. "Come on. We've got some planning to do. Bring the milk."

"What?"

"Mrs. Shaw. Trust me."

I stomp my foot. "What did you call me?"

He grins. "You heard me, and you are absolutely right. We won't be married until tomorrow."

David leads me down the hallway, past Michael and Mollie, who are in a huddle at the kitchen table, then out the front door. He proceeds to cross the street toward his car.

"What are you doing?"

He opens the passenger door and waves me in. "You'll see."

It's obvious he's not going to let me out of this, so I might as well play along. "The mall?"

David laughs as he settles into his seat then drops the cookie bag in my lap and grabs the gallon of milk. He removes the lid and takes a long swig straight from the jug before handing it back to me. "Ahh. That tastes good. You should help yourself."

"No thanks. I'm not going to swap spit with you."

"Maybe after we're married." His eyes twinkle.

"Where are we going?"

"Three important places."

I slide my feet up on his dash. Not that I would admit it to him, but his car is one sick ride. While he speeds down the road, I lay my head back on the headrest as I hold on to the gallon of milk, condensation dripping down my leg. No matter how much I complain, it's not going to change things, so I should just let him do whatever he has planned.

He screeches to a halt in front of Dragon Park, the neighborhood play area that has a massive concrete-and-mosaic dragon popping in and out of the ground all around the playground equipment. When we were little, we spent countless hours climbing on the dragon, but that was a long time ago. It's been ages since I told my concrete mosaic friend my secrets and dreams.

"Petie."

"Yep. Petie. I thought he needed to witness this."

I cut my eyes toward him. "Witness what?"

He motions with his head. "You'll see. Come on."

I leave the gallon of milk in his car and follow him. He climbs the dragon's tail with me right behind. He makes it to the first hump before he slides down Petie's back to the sandy ground below.

I hover over him. "You never could make it past his first hump."

David holds his arms out. "Wanna help me up?"

I shake my head. "Nuh-uh. Not falling for that. You've pulled that one on me too many times."

He clutches his chest with his hands. "Don't you trust me?"

"Not at all." I sit on the hump as David crawls on his knees to kneel in front of me. "Fine, I'll do this right here."

Uh-oh.

He digs in his front pocket and retrieves a small velvet bag. He clears his throat and pulls out a ring. My heart sinks, and I can't find my voice. I can't even find my breath.

"Mackenzie Grace Hamilton, will you fake marry me?"

He holds out a ring, and I squeeze my knees together to keep from falling off Petie.

"What is that?"

David blushes. "My dad gave my mom this as a promise ring when they were in high school." He lets out a nervous chuckle. "I know it's pretty cheesy, but..."

My jaw drops. "I can't take that. It's not right." *His mother was pretty in every way.*

He waves it in front of me. "Please. She loved you, and... well, she was such a jokester. She'd get a kick out of this project." He looks up at the sky, and his eyes sparkle, maybe from amusement but probably from a smattering of tears. "I know she's watching and laughing at us." He glances back at me. "Please take it. You can give it back to me when the project is over."

If he weren't so damn ugly, I would smother his face with kisses. That's the most romantic thing any guy has ever done for me. When I can breathe again, I clear my throat and whisper, "Okay."

I hold out my left hand, and he slides it onto my ring finger.

"Thank you." With a sly grin, he adds, "Do I get a kiss now?"

He scoots closer to me, and I shove him away. I wobble before I fall into the sandpit next to him, barely missing his right arm. "Don't push it, mister."

Petie was stop number one. No telling what else Mr. Shaw has up his sleeve. Forget about surviving the next four weeks. I hope I make it through the night.

Chapter 8

By the way she guzzles the milk straight out of the carton like a dude, I know Kenzie is freaking out pretty bad because of my proposal. Even though it is just a silly project for school, I was sincere. I would throw away my teenage bro card and marry her today if she'd let me. But I need to lighten up, or else she's going to get dehydrated from all the sweat pouring onto my passenger seat.

"Why don't you do our 'how do you see each other' sheet while I drive to stop number two? It will give you something to focus on instead of that rock on your hand."

She peers down at her left hand, the light shimmering off my mother's promise ring. "I can't keep this. It's too... real."

I hold out my hand. "Okay, give it here."

Kenzie leans away from me, protecting her left hand with her entire body. "On second thought, I'll hold on to it for a while, as long as I get to fling it at your face when we call it quits."

That's the Kenzie I know. She's thrown everything from mud pies to her fist at me over the years, so slinging a ring in my face seems strangely natural. "I wouldn't have it any other way."

"Phooey. I forgot my packet."

I jerk my thumb to the back seat. "Lucky for me, I didn't."

She unbuckles her seatbelt and leans over with her butt practically in my face as she fishes out the packet from my book bag. *Have mercy.* When she plops back into her seat, she slides a dark strand of hair behind her ear as she flips through the pages, oblivious to the fact that my face is on fire.

"Let's see. Do I see you as tactful? Nope. Dominating? Hardly at all. Easygoing? Somewhat."

I harrumph. "Somewhat? I'm one hundred percent easygoing. You used to call me a wet noodle because I would go with the flow too much."

She snorts. "Times change. Are you confident? Totally. Selfish?" Kenzie stares out the window and chews on her bottom lip.

I turn down Hillsboro Road toward the church we attended as kids. "Well? Do you think I'm selfish?"

She shakes her head then clears her throat. While I drive, she doodles on my paper.

"What are you doing?"

"Shh." She draws boxes and adds text with bullet points. Kenzie shakes her head and scribbles through the diagram. "Never mind. I was trying to visualize the project. It's how my brain works."

"And I really appreciate the mess you made on *my* packet."

Kenzie chuckles then reads each question out loud and answers them with mostly truthful replies until she gets to the last question on the sheet. "Are you honest?"

I turn into the parking lot, pull up to the front of the church, and throw the car into park. "I've always been honest with you. That's all I ask in return."

Her mouth drops open. "I'm honest."

I slide out of the car and run around to open her door, but she bolts out of the car before I have the opportunity to be a gentleman. "I am as honest as I can be." She turns in circles in the church parking lot. "What are we doing here?"

"I was thinking we could put this down in our packet as where we got married."

"You are having way too much fun with this project." Her eyes roam up to the steeple as she points to the small, enclosed landing at the base. "As long as I get to throw my bouquet from that."

"As you wish," I say as I take a bow.

She plants her hands on her hips. "Quotes from *The Princess Bride* are not allowed, buster."

I hold my hands out in defense. "It fit the situation. But I'll try to be good. Let's go."

Since she doesn't seem to care, I skip the part about being a gentleman this time. Before she takes one step, I already have the car cranked. She drags her heels getting back to my car as if she's lost in thought. "Where are you taking me next? Our honeymoon destination?"

My smile fades, and panic races across her face.

"Oh my God. You were, weren't you?"

I rest my head on the steering wheel, feeling as deflated as Fiona's old swim floaties. "Maybe."

She giggles. "You are so predictable. Can we go home now?"

"Nope. One more stop."

"If you say the first home we'll buy, I might throw up on you."

Dammit. "Never mind."

I DON'T EVEN GET MY Mustang in park before Kenzie jumps out and runs across the street to her house, still clinging to the gallon jug of milk. It doesn't take me long to catch up to her with my long stride.

"Kenz, we're not done for tonight."

Without slowing down, she yells over her shoulder, "Yes, we are!"

I grab her arm, and like a boomerang, she catapults back toward me. She plants her hands on my chest to keep from slamming into me.

After I work up the courage, I say, "I need to ask a favor."

With fire in her eyes, she replies, "No."

"You haven't even heard me out."

Kenzie jerks away from me and groans. "There is nothing I can do for you."

I take her by the arm and lead her to the steps on her porch. Running a hand through my hair, I stall, trying to find the right words. I squeeze my eyes shut and ask, "Do you know anything about website design?"

"Why?"

She'll never understand, but I have to try. "I really need to get this scholarship, but it requires I submit a website. I don't have a clue where to start."

Kenzie cocks her head to the side and, for the slightest moment, gives me confidence she's going to say she'll help me. She chews her lip before she replies. "What's the topic?"

A glimmer of hope springs through my chest. "It's for my band, and I—"

"Not a chance."

She jumps up and bolts through the door past the kitchen table, where Michael, Mollie, and Mrs. Hamilton sit. Kenzie barrels down the hallway toward her bedroom. Standing in the middle of the kitchen, I scrub my face with my hand. That didn't work out like I hoped.

"Having fun?" Hamilton's mischievous grin needs to be smacked off his face, and if his mother weren't sitting there, I probably would have done so.

Thank goodness Mollie reads my mind because she swats him on the shoulder. "Not nice."

He slinks away from her. "What? He knew to let her warm up to the idea of him being her faux husband." He shakes his head at me. "Dude, you have got to learn what makes her tick."

Mrs. Hamilton pops him on the other shoulder. "Michael, I think it's wonderful that David is hooked up with Kenzie on this project."

Heat rises from my face and shoots out my ears. Mollie gasps, and Michael rests his head on the kitchen table.

"Mom, don't say 'hooked up' when you're talking about your daughter," he said.

She crunches her eyebrows together. "Is that bad?"

I nod. "Yes, ma'am."

She ruffles my hair like she's done every day for the past ten years. "You're a fine boy. I'm sure if my Kenzie hooked up with you, it couldn't be bad."

"Mom! Stop. Please."

Mollie jumps out of her chair. "I better check on Kenz. Later, hubby."

"Later, honey-kins."

Blech.

Mrs. Hamilton's phone rings, and she smiles. "I better take this." She heads to her room as I slouch into a chair next to Hamilton.

"Awkward."

He shakes his head. "Ever since she's been dating this latest guy, she says the craziest stuff."

"How is Collin, the poet?"

Hamilton shoves the project packet into his backpack and zips it shut. "He's all right, but Kenzie still hangs on to the idea that Mom and Dad are going to get back together. It's not going to happen. Dad has moved on, and Mom seems happy, and it sure beats having them under the same roof, yelling at each other all the time."

My mouth turns down. "I'd take yelling any day of the week."

Hamilton sighs. "Man, that was a sucky thing for me to say. I'm sorry."

I shrug. "It's okay, but I think Dad's stuck. He won't move on, and it's hard." A lump forms in my throat. I hate talking about my dad's chronic sadness, but it bleeds over into Fi's and my mood, making us one big house full of mopey humans.

"I know. I'm sure all this fake wedding stuff has got to be hard on you. I didn't even think about it until now."

I wave him off. "It's fine. My parents had a perfect marriage. Way too short, but what time they had was... it was great."

Memories flood my brain: trips to the beach, baseball games, Christmas mornings—all good. I don't remember anything bad until she started her treatments. And even then, it wasn't bad, only very sad.

Before my emotions get the best of me, I stand to leave. Mrs. Hamilton reenters the room all smiles.

"Oh, David, I have something for you."

She rushes to the refrigerator and pulls out a casserole dish. "I know your dad likes my lasagna, so I made a double batch."

I kiss her cheek as I take the dish from her like I've done so many times over the years. When Hamilton isn't watching, she places a twenty-dollar bill in my hand. I shake my head, but she gives me one of her it's-not-up-for-debate expressions. If it weren't for her, I'd have run out of gas a dozen times in the last year.

"Thank you," I whisper.

With a thousand thoughts consuming my brain, I walk across the street and find my father doing what he does best: helping Fiona with her math homework. Both of their noses work overtime when they smell the Italian dish in my hands.

"Woo-hoo! I love Mrs. Hamilton's lasagna." Fiona doesn't yet understand how hard it is for Dad to accept help. She only knows a good, home-cooked meal when she smells one.

Dad's turned-down mouth lets me know he wishes Mrs. Hamilton hadn't done it.

"Before you ask, I tried not to accept, but you know how she is."

"I know." He blows out a large breath.

Fiona runs back into the living room with plates and forks, and we dive into our meal. For the next ten minutes, the only sounds in our house are the moans and groans from the three of us as we devour the lasagna. It hits the spot, as usual. Dad wants us to eat healthily, but he's so busy with work and being two parents, it doesn't leave much room for home-cooked meals.

"I got an email from one of your teachers about a project. What's that all about?" he asks between bites.

Fiona quirks an eyebrow.

"Yeah. I got lucky. I guess it could have been worse."

"What's your project?" Fiona gulps down her iced tea.

I really don't want to talk about it anymore, but stalling won't stop their inquiry. "A pretend marriage for a month."

Fiona giggles, and I tickle her stomach.

"It's an experiment to see how compatible we are, if we can work together, learn to live on a budget. Stuff like that."

Fiona stuffs her mouth with another bite, the cheese clinging to the fork. "Who is your partner?"

Dad's eyes twinkle. Mama always said I had his eyes.

"Uh, I got Kenzie."

She grins like she won a blue ribbon. "Does that mean she'll be living with us?"

"No!" Heat rushes up my neck and makes my ears burn. That's happened a lot today. "I mean, it's not like that. It's pretend. Besides, Kenzie isn't all that excited about having to work with me."

Dad picks up our empty, sauce-smeared plates and stacks them. "She'll come around."

I glance at my feet. "Dad, I did something without asking you, and you can be mad if you want. It's not a permanent thing."

He stands still, waiting for me to continue.

"The first thing we were supposed to do was get a ring for our spouse. So, I, uh... borrowed Mom's promise ring. I know I should have asked first, but you weren't home. I'm sure Kenzie will take care of it. Plus, I'll get it back when the project is over."

He places a hand over mine. "It's okay. If it was anyone besides Mackenzie, it would have bothered me. But Vanessa loved Kenzie like one of her own." He grins. "I bet she's enjoying this project."

Fiona nods.

"I think so too." I can almost see Mom giggling about it.

Dad sits back on the couch and pats his full belly. "I hope Kenzie warms up to you again. I don't know what happened, but I see the hurt in your eyes when she gives you the cold shoulder."

"Me, too, Dad." At this point, I'd settle for a lukewarm shoulder.

Chapter 9

Mollie doesn't even bother knocking on my bedroom door. As usual, she makes herself at home in my room, stealing my Cheetos. Good thing we've been friends since kindergarten because, with the mood I'm in, any other person would get a major tongue lashing. After the day I've had, only Mollie could get away with barging in like that.

She sits on the edge of my bed while we watch *The Princess Bride* for the umpteenth time. The title has a nice variety of colors and no clashing combinations, so again, it proves my color theory.

"How did you get so lucky to be paired with Michael?" I dive my chopsticks into the Cheetos bag to snag one. It might take longer to eat this way, but I don't have to lick the orange dust off my fingers.

She drops her handful of Cheetos onto the floor. While she licks the orange residue from each finger, her face glows red. "I don't know but, man oh man, am I ever glad. Half the boys in our class don't even know I exist, and the others are icky. Any of them would have been awkward."

I huff. "Not as awkward as my partner."

She shoves my shoulder, toppling me over the side of the bed. "Girl, you are an idiot. He's a babe, and he's nice. Oh, and there's one other thing. He's got it soooo bad for you."

I roll my eyes. "No, he doesn't. Besides, we're not compatible, and this project will confirm everything I already know."

She snatches the cheese puffs bag from me and dives in for another handful. "You should have heard Harper complaining about you in AP English." She wrinkles her nose, doing a perfect impression of Harper. In a high-pitched voice, she mimics our local mean girl. "She's in this class for *one* day, and she gets my boyfriend for a partner."

I belt out a laugh, and Mollie coughs on Cheetos dust. "Funny how she's the only one who still thinks they're together."

She shushes me as Inigo Montoya says his famous line. And like we've never watched that scene before, we sit in silence as Inigo sword fights Count Rugen. Together, we yell with Inigo that he wants his father back.

Mollie collapses onto the bed, and we both breathe like we've been involved in the sword fight right alongside Inigo.

"I love that scene."

"Yep. Pretty awesome."

With her knee, Mollie taps mine. "I think you're waiting for your one true love." She draws out "true love" like Westley did when he was mostly dead.

"What's wrong with that?"

She shrugs. "Nothing. But don't be surprised if you can't see the trees for the forest."

I scrunch up my eyebrows. "Don't you have that turned around?"

She shakes her head. "Nope. Think about it."

We fall into a comfortable silence as Westley reunites with Princess Buttercup and they ride off into the sunset. The kissing scene gets me. Every. Single. Time. We both let out sighs. "Epic."

"Yep." Then she adds, "What kind of ring is Michael going to get me?"

"I have no idea, but it will be interesting. That's for sure. Don't expect it to be fancy."

She holds up my hand. "Like this sweet ring you got from David? My gosh. It's real, isn't it?"

I can't help but grin when the ring sparkles in the light. "Yeah. It was his mother's. It even has his parents' names engraved on the sides."

She clutches her chest. "Aww. The two hearts joined in the middle is so romantic."

I roll my eyes. "It's sweet, but I think he went with the easiest option."

She grabs my hand. "If you don't appreciate it, I'll take it."

She does her best to pry it off my finger, but in a fit of giggles, I wrestle my arm free.

"I didn't say that. It's beautiful, but I didn't see it coming. He did a fake proposal and everything. At Petie's, of all places."

Mollie turns my hand in different directions, letting the light reflect off the tiny diamond. "You are such an idiot. He never would have done that if Tiffany was his partner."

"I can't explain—"

She holds out a hand for me to stop. "I don't want to hear an explanation. I can't change your oddness, but promise me one thing."

I growl. "What?"

"Be kind. He really is a nice guy."

I point my finger at her. "For you. When this is over, and I can say, 'I told you so,' you are going to owe me something. Not sure what that will be yet, but it will be big."

She grabs another handful of Cheetos as I dive in again with my chopsticks. "And you will owe *me* when *I'm* right."

A familiar knock rattles the door. Our knock, knock-knock, knock-knock-knock from when we were kids tells me it's Michael. David used to do it, too, but he stopped rapping on my door a long time ago. Mollie jumps up and licks the remainder of the orange Cheetos dust off her fingers. She runs a hand through her auburn hair and checks her shirt, which is covered with orange powder. She grabs a pillow and places it over her chest.

"Enter, Sir Michael."

Michael opens the door, and a cheesy grin spreads across his face. "Good evening, ladies. I need to steal my bride away so we can finish our homework."

Mollie blushes and stifles a giggle. I shoo them out of my room. "Go. If you hurt my best friend, I'll tell all of your horrible toddler secrets."

"You wouldn't."

"Try me."

Mollie darts out of the room. Michael shakes his head, but satisfaction plays over his face. He leans against the doorframe and crosses his arms over his chest.

When he doesn't move, I say, "Go on and say it. I know you have something on your mind, so spit it out."

"You need to call David to finish your project. That was rude of you to leave him like that."

"Yes, Father. First, it's this project, and now he wants help with a website to get a scholarship."

As if a light bulb goes off in his head, he says, "So that's why. He asked me, but I only deal with zeros and ones."

"Well, I'm not doing it."

Michael crosses his arms. "Sis, if he needs it to go to college, help the guy out. You know you can do it."

"Harrumph."

"Could you live with yourself if you found out he wasn't able to go to college because he didn't get a scholarship and all that stood in the way was *you* not helping? You know money is tight for them."

At birth, our mother gave Michael the guilt gene, and he uses it on me every chance he gets. Like the time we were five and we spilled my mother's red nail polish on the beige carpet. We hid it with a stack of magazines, but he got all twitchy and confessed.

I blow the hair out of my eyes. "I'll think about it."

Michael winks at me. "Thanks. I better go spend time with my wife before she trades me in for a more attentive model."

"Ha. Not hardly." I throw a pillow at him. He ducks, and the pillow hits the door as he closes it.

Ugh. I know he's right. I'm being stupid. Just because we aren't ever going to be a couple in real life doesn't mean I can't work on this stupid project with him. It's only a class assignment. I can do this. All I have to do is pretend his name is something else, like Mitch or Aiden. Both are pretty names. I pull out my phone and dial his number.

"Hello, Mrs. Shaw."

"Stop calling me that."

His deep, rumbling laughter sends a trembly sensation down my spine that I didn't expect.

"I take it back. You can call me Mrs. Shaw if you'll let me call you Aiden."

"What?"

"I like the name Aiden. You look like an Aiden, so from now on, I'm going to call you Aiden."

More rumbly laughter. "If that's all it takes for you to share the same space with me for more than five minutes at a time, you can call me Prince Humperdinck if you want."

That was too easy. I should have made my demands more difficult. "Uh... okay then. Do you want to finish tonight's assignment? I think we can complete it over the phone."

"I've got a better idea. Come over here."

Nope, nope. Not gonna happen.

"Uh..."

"The door's already open. I'm waiting..."

I fake a yawn. "Come to think of it, I'm really tired."

"Get your butt over here, Mrs. Shaw, or I'm going to have to show you who wears the pants in this family."

I'm going to bite my lip in two trying not to laugh. "You wouldn't dare."

"I'm in the middle of the street now."

"You better not—"

"I'm in your front yard. Look out your window."

Crap. I sneak a peek out my window right as he waves at me. *Double crap.* "I think I'll have to get a restraining order on you."

"Nonsense. I only want quality time with my wife."

He is impossible and enjoying this way too much. After stalling for as long as I can, I let out a sigh. "Fine." I click my phone off and huff while I walk outside to where he waits under the huge magnolia tree, looking all too satisfied with himself.

"Your choice. Do you want to work in my room, where there's a good chance of Fiona bugging the crap out of us every two minutes, or do you want to go to the Donut Den and finish this over some coffee? My treat."

My pulse quickens with the thought of being in his room. I haven't been there in years. In fact, other than Michael's, I haven't been in a boy's room ever. So, yeah. Awkward. But the thought of seeing Fiona does make me giddy. I adore his little sister, and it's been ages since I spent time with her. When I put my self-imposed David ban in place, she was collateral damage. But David knows I can be won over any day of the week by a cinnamon powdered donut and a caramel latte. *Dang it.* My treacherous stomach growls, and by the impish grin that grows on his face, he heard it.

"I guess your answer is the Den."

"I hate you." I stomp past him across the street and toward his car.

He rushes to catch up and gives my ponytail a slight tug. "Love, hate... it's a fine line between the two, don't you think?"

I give his shoulder a playful shove. "You really shouldn't read all those romance novels."

He opens the car door for me, and after I settle in, he slams it shut then leans in the open window, his face inches from mine. "Maybe you should read more of them." He pinches my cheek and snatches his hand away before I can smack it. He is so annoying.

Chapter 10

She is so absolutely adorable in a quirky kind of way, and I'm thanking the homework gods that I got paired with Kenzie. She wants to call me Aiden. I have no idea what that's all about, but she can call me Beelzebub for all I care as long as she talks to me.

"What question are we on?"

She shakes her head. "Nope. Not until my tummy is full. You promised."

"You should have eaten some of the lasagna your mother made. Delicious as always."

She stares out the window of my car. "I wasn't hungry at the time."

I poke at her stomach, and she swats my hand away. "You were holding out for a Donut Den run, weren't you?"

Kenzie juts her chin a little higher. "Was not."

"Were, too, and it worked. You wore me down with your one-track mind."

She rolls her eyes.

I point my finger at her. "You've already got this wife thing all figured out."

She snorts. "Hardly. I seriously doubt anyone will ever call me 'wife' in real life. I'm way too abnormal."

I pull into the parking lot and find a space near the entrance. "You think that's a bad thing. Abnormal is where it's at. Who wants plain vanilla when you can have... cinnamon?"

"Speaking of cinnamon, let's go. You owe me something." With our project packet in one hand, she opens the car door and marches toward the front counter like she owns the place. She doesn't even have to tell Reggie, the owner of the shop, what she wants. It's been her standard order since we started coming here. At first, we would visit the mom-and-pop shop after soccer games and for birthday parties. Then it became the after-school hangout.

It all changed when she stopped coming with me. I know she still stops by, because every time I am at her house, hanging out with Michael, I smell cinnamon when I walk down the hall, and she has never been able to wipe the powdery mustache evidence off her face before I notice it.

Reggie plunks two in a bag and waits for my order.

Unlike Kenzie, I like to order something different each time. I tap a finger to my chin. "How about a blueberry-glazed donut and two caramel coffees, please?"

Kenzie scrunches her face. "Blueberry? What is wrong with you?"

"It's good. I'll let you try some of mine."

She shakes her head. "No thanks."

"Come on. Married couples eat off each other's plates all the time."

She swallows hard, and Reggie gives me a what-the-heck expression.

"Not this couple."

Reggie adds my donut to the bag, and while he pours our coffees, she sniffs inside the bag. "Your blueberry donut is overpowering my cinnamon ones."

"Is this a you-got-peanut-butter-on-my-chocolate situation?"

She giggles, thinking back to one of our favorite Reese's Peanut Butter Cups commercials as kids. "I guess so."

Kenzie finds a booth in the back corner while I pay for our food. I'm not sure if she wants privacy or if she's embarrassed to be seen with me. Either way, I like having her to myself for a few minutes, especially when her shoulders aren't so kinked up, so maybe she's relaxing a bit around me. Hamilton probably gave her a stern talking-to about this being a class project and to suck it up. Whatever the reason, I'm just happy she has to hang with me for a while. My only fear is that I'll get used to it, and when the assignment is over, she'll pull up those walls around her again.

I slide into the booth next to her, and she scoots as far away from me as possible, scrunching up against the wall. "What are you doing?"

"Homework. I can't see what you're working on from across the table."

I hand her the bag, and she extracts our donuts. With a prune face, she hands me mine.

"Want to try it?"

"No thanks. I'll stick to my tried-and-true."

"Suit yourself." I throw the entire donut in my mouth and toss back some coffee. "Ahh. That is so good."

"Did you even taste it?"

"Yep." I point to the assignment. "What's next in the packet?"

She fumbles through the pages and taps her pencil on the "what do you want in a partner" page. "What are your top ten characteristics? Let me guess. Good-looking, popular, talkative, affectionate..."

I snatch the paper out of her hand. "Give me that." As I read over the list, she drums her fingers on the table. "Really? Out of everything on the list, you think those are most important to me?"

She nibbles on her donut, the dusty cinnamon sticking to her fingers. "So, if they aren't, then what are they?"

"You got one of them right."

She snaps her fingers in my face. "Ha! See, I know you."

I lean close to her, and the cinnamon-donut aroma tickles my nose. "Affectionate. I won't lie about that one. Who wouldn't want that? But that's not number one."

She rolls her eyes as she takes a swig from her coffee cup. "What is, Mr. Shaw?"

I'm digging the hint of a twinkle in her eye. "Honesty. I want a partner who is honest with me at all times, no matter how cruel it will be."

She swallows her coffee and looks down at the paper. "How... honest are you being?"

I snatch her donut out of her hand and hold it high over my head. "I am being completely honest. And if you don't answer the question honestly, I will eat your donut."

Fire shows in her eyes. "Don't do it." She stands in the booth to grab for the donut.

I hold it out of her reach, so she climbs over me to get to it. I take the opportunity to tickle her stomach, making her fall into my lap.

"Give it back." Her mouth forms a straight line, but a tinge of a smile appears.

"Be honest, Mrs. Shaw, or it's going in my mouth."

"Thoughtful, okay? My number one answer is thoughtful."

Our eyes meet, and for the slightest second, hers flick to my mouth, then back up to my eyes. She clears her throat, and in a whisper, she says, "Can I have my donut now?"

I mull over my answer. "The thoughtful thing to do would be to give it to you."

Still sitting in my lap, she holds out her hand for her donut. Instead of giving it to her, I feed it to her. A trail of cinnamon powder dusts her lips, and I wipe it off with my thumb.

"How thoughtful of you," she croaks as if it's hard to form words.

"Look at you, being all honest and stuff." I wink at her.

She pinches my shoulder just as a huge gasp comes from behind my head. "Oh my gawd. Get out of my boyfriend's lap."

I jerk my head around to see the she-devil herself. Tiffany's arms are crossed so tight across her chest she's going to give herself the Heimlich.

And that toe-tapping needs to stop. Instead of releasing Kenzie, I slide my hands up her back to pull her closer. Kenzie stiffens, and I swear I hear Tiffany growl.

Barely above a whisper, Kenzie says, "Let me go."

I take a deep breath and hold my hands over my head so Kenzie can climb off my lap, almost hitting the family jewels in the process.

Tiffany cocks her head to the side. "Kenz, leave him alone. He doesn't like you like that. It's a class project, and he will do anything to get a good grade."

An evil grin grows on Kenzie's face, one that I haven't seen in very long time. She holds out her left hand, the one with my mother's ring on it, so Tiffany and her posse can see it. "You might be right about that, Tif, but at least I got this to show for my pain and suffering."

Tiffany yanks Kenzie by the hand until she's back into my lap. "What the frig is this?"

"It's called a promise ring. Real diamonds, white gold, and it's even engraved. So romantic." Kenzie's smile twinkles brighter than the ring. "What did Rhett get you?"

Tif shoves Kenzie's hand away and narrows her stare at me. "You gave her a real ring?"

As if Kenzie can read my mind, we both nod at the same time before I say, "Oh, it's real. My dad bought it for my mother when they were about my age."

Tiffany rolls her eyes. "So it's old."

"More like one of a kind." Kenzie holds out her hand to observe the ring once again. "Only someone who is... thoughtful would give their partner something like this."

I belt out a laugh and fist bump Kenzie. We clink coffee cups, making Tiffany fume.

"Take it off."

Kenzie spits out a sip of coffee, making Tiffany jump back to avoid getting sprayed. "Excuse me?"

Tiffany inspects her shirt for spew before saying, "Take it off. You can't wear real jewelry given to you by *my* boyfriend."

I stand up then turn to face Tiffany. I put a hand on each of her shoulders. "Look, Tif. We went on one date. One. And that was under extreme duress. Don't make it out to be more than it was. I am not your boyfriend and never have been."

She swats my hands off her shoulders and turns her wrath on Kenzie. "This isn't over." She looks at her two pals. "Come on, girls. This place stinks." Over her shoulder, Tiffany adds, "By the way, if you *ever* give me something like that, I will throw it in the Cumberland River."

"Don't hold your breath."

When she slams the door so hard it makes the clock on the wall wobble, I dare a peek at Kenzie.

She bites her lip as she writes something down in our packet. "You sure know how to pick 'em, don't you?"

I slink back into the seat beside her and rest my head on the table to let out a groan. "She is not my girlfriend. I lost a bet, okay? You happy?"

When I get the nerve to look at her, I expect her to be laughing at me, but what I get is a stoic face, as if she's trying to process my words.

"She's not the girl for me, Kenzie. That's not what I like. You know me better than anyone, or at least I thought you did."

"I know." She lets out a giggle. "I do love to make her squirm though." Kenzie holds out her left hand and admires the ring. "It is pretty. I'd never deserve anything so beautiful."

I snap my head up off the table. "I think you make it beautiful." I look around the room, suddenly very uncomfortable in my skin. "Uh... I think we should call it a night."

She shoves all the pages together and nods. "Good idea."

Through the awkward silence on the short drive back to my house, my car's rumbly muffler echoes through my brain. I pull into my driveway, and I clear my throat to prepare for another attempt to get her to help me with my application.

"I have a proposal for you."

Kenzie holds out her right hand. "Does it involve bling for this hand?"

I throw my head back and chuckle. "No, but if you have any web design experience, I would really, really appreciate the help. Kenz, I need this."

Kenzie stares out her window, so I continue.

"And if you help me get something epic to submit... I'll finish the marriage project on my own."

Her head snaps around so fast her hair whips into her face. "What?"

I nod. "If you help me, I will finish the project."

She stares a hole in me. "What's the catch?"

Of course she thinks there's a catch. Kenzie has to learn to trust me again. "As soon as I have something to submit, something that will blow them away, you won't have to do any more on our project. I promise."

She chews her lip as she ponders my offer. "So, the faster I do your website, the faster I will be done with the school project. Is that right?"

I nod. "But it has to be good. They only award one scholarship, and with the way things are at home..."

"I'll do it."

My head snaps in her direction. I can't believe my ears. "Seriously?"

"Yeah. I can't promise it will be scholarship worthy, but I'll do my best." She flashes me a one-second smile before she focuses out the window again.

"Thank you."

She shrugs as she starts across the street to her house. When I follow her, she waves me off. "I'm a big girl. I'll see you tomorrow in class. And I'll give some thought to your website. See you later, Aiden."

I chuckle. "Anytime, Mrs. Shaw."

The streetlight casts a long shadow of my body as I stand in the middle of the road, watching her until she is safely inside her home. Right when I turn to go toward my house, I see the slightest movement in Kenzie's room. If I didn't know better, I would think she's watching me from behind her curtains.

I could get used to this side of Kenzie. I dare not wave, because the last thing I want to do is to go backward in our friendship. In two days, we've made two giant steps forward. I don't want to do anything to send her running away from me again.

Chapter 11

While Michael drives us to school, I sneak peeks at the ring on my finger that my faux husband gave me. Wearing something his dead mother owned kind of gives me the heebie-jeebies, but she was the kindest lady I ever knew, and I'm sure she wouldn't mind. And her name was so pretty. I'll never forget how jovial she was all the time, and it rubbed off on her family. Even when she got sick, she never went without a smile, at least when I was around. Mom would bake her anything she wanted, anything that she had a "hankering" for, in her words. My job was to deliver the baked goods and to keep David and Fiona from slipping into a dark hole of depression. Poor Fiona was so little when she lost her mother. I bet she hardly remembers her.

"David set the bar high for all of us losers." Michael shifts gears as we roll into the school parking lot.

"That's your problem, not mine." I turn my hand in different directions, letting the sunlight twinkle off the small diamonds. "But it is pretty. Prettier than I'll ever have in real life."

He swings into a parking space and turns off the truck. "Yeah, enjoy it while it lasts."

I gasp. "Hey now. I'm not that bad, am I?"

He raises an eyebrow. "Sis, you determine who is 'good' by the colors of the letters in their name. Who does that?"

I snarl at him. "It works, and this project is going to prove my theory. You're just jealous that you have to wade through the shark-infested waters, finding people you can count on. I don't have to do that." I smile super big. "It makes life so much easier."

Although David gave me the prettiest ring, he's still in the ugly category. I'm not going to focus on a tiny flaw in my system. It's one little fluke, and if Michael doesn't figure that out, I am definitely not going to mention it.

He rolls his eyes. "You are so weird."

I jump out of the truck and grab my backpack. "So, I've been told. Weird is fine with me."

"Good."

"Good."

"Great."

I shove his arm. "Stop it."

"Stop it."

"Ugh." I swing around to face him. "Don't say it."

He holds his hands out in surrender. "I wasn't going to say anything else."

I jut my chin high. "And for your information, I agreed to help Aiden with his web page."

He raises an eyebrow. "Who is Aiden?"

I wave my hand in the air. "Aiden is David. Don't ask. The point is he agreed to let me off the hook on this marriage mess in exchange for a top-notch web page."

"Really?"

I grin. "Yep."

"I didn't know you had web design skills."

"I may not know the inner workings of a computer, and I certainly don't know how to make the power go off during the ACT exam like some certain person who will go unnamed, but I know my way around designing a page."

He gasps. "You think I was the one who made the power go off?"

"Who else could it have been?"

Michael taps his finger to his chin. "Maybe it was a coincidence."

I snicker. "Of course. Anyway, as soon as I have the web page ready for him to submit, he'll take over the marriage project all by himself. Easy peasy."

He stares away. "Hmm. Interesting. Sounds like you're both winners."

"Exactly."

He points behind me. "Here come the sharks."

I peer over my shoulder to where Tiffany and Harper stand on the sidewalk, eyes narrowed, virtual darts being thrown in my direction. I shake my head. "Can't they get it through their thick skulls that I don't want him?"

He leans down to whisper in my ear, his words meant only for me. "It's not what you want. It's what *he* wants. And that ticks her off."

"Ugh, you are worse than Aiden-David is. See you in first period."

I stomp off toward my locker with Tiffany and company right on my heels. If the clickity-click of her shoes didn't tip me off, it would have been the gag-inducing perfume cloud surrounding her. Trying my best to ignore both, I dig around in my locker, hoping she passes on by. When I close my locker, I notice her on the other side of the hallway, tapping her toe.

"What?" I make a point to run my hand with the promise ring through my hair. At this point, I don't care if I'm rubbing it in.

"Don't get so comfortable with that... relic on your finger. It doesn't mean a thing."

I admire the ring while her face turns a dangerous shade of red. "Riiiiight. That's why you are making such a fuss. See you in class."

Homeroom isn't much better. Every girl has to see the ring and hear about how he gave it to me. But the worst part is every girl tells me how lucky I am to have David as a partner. *He's so great. He's so sweet. He's so cute. He's so hot.* Gross. The only thing I can do is grit my teeth and smile. Ten more minutes before I have to face him, and no telling what Mr. Carter has up his sleeve today.

This is the beginning of a very long, agonizing semester. I should have left my schedule the way it was. As soon as I get home, I'm going to knock out that web page so I can be finished with David once and for all.

HERE GOES NOTHING. The minute I walk into first period, my eyes land on David, or at least as much as I can see of him over the gaggle of chicks swarming him, giving him the third degree about the ring. When he sees me standing at the door, he has a help-me expression on his face. *Poor baby.* That's what he gets for making a huge public display of affection over a stupid project. Of course someone would be lurking to post it on social media. Next time, he should just give me a hair tie for a ring, not that there will be a next time.

Crap. Hanging out with him is turning me into a softie.

"Guys, give him some air." I shoo them with my hands as if they're flies. And with the sweetest voice that almost gives me a cavity, I ask, "Honey, are they bothering you?"

The corners of his eyes crinkle when he smiles up at me. "Yes, they are. They can't take no for an answer. You better be good to me, or there will be a lot of competition to take your place."

He winks, and I stick my tongue out at him in response. They grumble but scramble when Mr. Carter enters the room dressed like a priest. *Oh my gosh!*

I slink into the desk behind David and dare another glance at my pretty ring. I wonder what it was like when Mrs. Shaw got it from David's father. Every time I saw the two together, they acted like newlyweds, a far cry from my parents. Mine always act like they can't stand to breathe the same air. Maybe this ring is magical.

Mr. Carter clears his throat, and giggles erupt throughout the class. "Now, now. I know I don't make a really good man of the cloth, but since we are going to have our pretend wedding ceremony, I thought I would at least look the part."

A bead of sweat trickles between my boobs. I figured we would sign the marriage document in our packet and be done with it, but this is going too far. This is so not good.

"Hey, Dylan, why didn't you get your mom to officiate the weddings?" Harper giggles, thinking her question is hilarious.

Dylan glowers at her. "Do you want to be stuck with me for good? Legally? 'Cause she has the authority."

Harper's stupid grin fades, and if I could lunge over to his desk and hug him without making a fool of myself, I would.

"Dudes, can all of you come to the front of the class? Except for Eli. You're the other partner in your case."

Charlie blows him a kiss as he stands up with the other guys. Eli, being the jokester that he is, pretends to catch the kiss and stuff it in his pocket.

All the guys stand at the front with Mr. Carter in the middle. "Okay, ladies... and Eli. Find your partner."

Chairs scratch against the floor as the other half of the room moves about the class until they are all in front of their project partners. All except me. I freeze in my seat. David motions with his head to join him. I shake my head as another bead of sweat trickles down my neck.

"Ahh, she's got cold feet. I'll marry you." Tiffany bats her eyelashes at him.

I turn to Michael for help, but he's having too much fun chatting it up with Mollie. I stand and walk like my feet are encased in concrete.

David holds out his hand to take mine. "There you are, my blushing bride."

Tiffany sneers. As Rhett plays with a lock of her hair, she smacks his hand away.

"Calm down, tiger. You should be thanking your lucky stars you got partnered with me." Rhett winks at her.

Tiffany does a full-body shiver. "Ugh. Just don't touch me."

He shakes his head. "That's not part of the prenup."

Dylan, Harper's partner, high-fives Rhett.

Harper's nose scrunches as she takes a whiff of Dylan. "Don't you hate smelling like last week's garbage?"

He takes his Nirvana infatuation so far that he even wants to smell like a rock star. I always know when he arrives for band practice by the cloud of funk permeating the house.

He raises his arm close to her face, making her squeal. "I'd rather be hated for who I am than loved for who I'm not."

Rhett groans. "Dude, you are not the incarnation of Kurt Cobain, so stop it."

Dylan stalks over to Rhett, slinging the hair out of his eyes. "You don't know that for sure. My mother said 'Come as You Are' was on the radio when she and my dad—"

"Okay, that's enough." Mr. Carter separates them. "Let's get started before we know any more details about the origins of Dylan Malone."

I stifle a giggle and glance up at David. He stares at the ceiling, a pink flush running down his neck. When Dylan gets on one of his Nirvana kicks, it's hard to reel him in. If he weren't such a good guitar player, I think Michael would have kicked him out of their band a long time ago. I like Dylan as much as possible, but his name has a wicked grouping with brown right next to pink, so it's really icky. And he does take the reincarnation of Kurt Cobain a bit too far sometimes.

Harper covers her face with her hands. "This can't be happening to me."

Dylan has the nerve to sweep a lock of her hair behind her ear. "Oh, it's happening."

David's chuckle rumbles out of his chest. He leans down and whispers in my ear. "See? You could have it worse."

I give him a gentle shove with my shoulder; however, he does have a point.

"Do all you guys have your rings?" Mr. Carter scans the room. All the guys, except for Eli, rummage through their pockets and pull out various items to be used for wedding rings. Charlie has matching fake tattoos to be used in place of rings, and Dylan, as expected, uses a piece of guitar string fashioned into a circle. David takes out two gold bands from his front jeans pocket, and I suck in a breath, as do Tiffany and Harper.

Tiffany storms over and snarls while she glares at the rings in David's hands. "First, a real ring then this?" She snarls at Rhett. "You better have something this good, or else."

Rhett holds up a simple silver band, fake, I'm sure. "This is a mood ring, and trust me, it's more for me than you, so please wear it at all times."

Mr. Carter laughs. "Okay, class. Do you promise to love, honor, cherish, blah blah blah till death, er, I mean till the project is over?"

Everyone grumbles, "Yes, sir."

David looks into my eyes and whispers, "Yes."

I swallow a lump in my throat as he slips the wedding ring on my finger next to the promise ring. It's too big for my finger, and I'll probably have to put tape around it to keep it from falling off. I bite my lip to keep from showing my real emotions. "It's pretty."

"Simple, but... you know."

"I know. It was your mom's. You shouldn't have."

To break the spell, I focus on the other girls in the class. Mollie receives a purple stretchy-band ring from Michael, and she beams with pride. He could have given her a paper ring from a cigar box, and she would have liked it because it came from my brother. Harper's red face makes me assume she doesn't appreciate Dylan's guitar-string ring.

"By the power vested in me as your licensed secondary education teacher, I pronounce all of you fake husbands and wives. You may now kiss your brides."

David's eyebrow quirks up. I give him a stern warning look. "Do you want me to get this union annulled before the ink is dry on the paper?"

Mr. Carter laughs. "I'm kidding. No PDA in the classroom."

David belts out a laugh. "I won't push it, but one day, you may beg me for a kiss."

I snort. "Keep dreaming, Aiden."

In a soft voice only meant for me, he whispers, "Oh, I do, Mrs. Shaw."

Mr. Carter claps his hands. "Okay, now that we have that out of the way, I need each pair to sign the agreement form and file it away with the packet you will turn in at the end of the project. The first order of business is to pick your careers. One person from each pairing will pull out a slip of paper from this box to determine what careers you and your partner will have to work with. Research these careers, and determine what incomes you'll have. You will use this information to find a place to live and create a budget. Next, you'll start working on how to assign chores around the house."

Dylan laughs. "That's easy. Harper will do all the chores while I make my living as a rock star on the road."

"Don't count on it," Harper replies, more interested in her nails than anything her faux husband has to say.

Mr. Carter shakes up the box. "Yeah, don't count on it, because famous rock star that dies at age twenty-seven is not one of the career choices for this project." He holds the box in front of Dylan and shakes it. "You go first."

Dylan stuffs his hand into the box, fishes around for a second, and retrieves a slip of paper. We all wait for him to unfold it like it's a fortune cookie. He groans. "I am the CEO of a bank, and my wife is a novelist."

Harper woo-hoos and struts up and down the aisle. "My husband is loaded."

Mr. Carter pats her shoulder. "That probably means he works fifty-plus hours a week, so you get to take care of all the chores."

Her face falls, but then her eyes light up. "I'll hire someone to do all the dirty work while I plot out my next romance novel. Plus, I won't have to look at his ugly mug all the time."

Mr. Carter points to her desk. "You can work that out with your spouse. Next." He scans the room, and everyone trains their eyes on the floor.

"David, why don't you pick for you and your partner?"

He stuffs his hand in the box and pulls out a slip of paper.

David grins when he reads our jobs. "We are the proud owners of a bakery. A dog bakery called the Barkery."

I slump into the nearest seat. My breakfast threatens to rise from my stomach. Michael's laughter from across the room breaks my spell. He gives me a thumbs-up. He knows how I don't like dogs. They are cute and fluffy and sweet, but the word... I can't deal with it.

Mr. Carter doesn't wait for me to recover before he moves on to the next couple. David takes me by the hand and leads me back to my desk. I plop down in the seat and stare at nothing in particular.

"This is good. You are a great baker, and I love dogs. I never knew anything like this actually existed." He pulls out his laptop from his book bag and taps away while I sit in silence.

Not only do I have to work with David, but now we have to run a dog bakery. This project is getting uglier by the minute.

Chapter 12

By the queasy expression on her face, Kenzie appears as if she swallowed a goat, but I try not to think about it while I search the Internet for dog bakeries. I wish she were as interested in this project as she is in biting all of her nails down to nubs.

"Did you know there aren't many dog bakeries in Nashville?" If I stick to facts, maybe she will reengage.

She stares at the rings on her left hand.

"The whole bakery idea is actually not so terrible. This business report shows Give a Dog a Bone tripled their sales last year by having a cart at Centennial Park. It's a great idea. Vendors are all over that place, selling human stuff, and dog owners walk their critters there. Hello? It's a no-brainer."

Nothing. Maybe I need to try a less-than-subtle approach to get her talking.

"I got arrested for speeding this morning. And I was naked. Texting while driving too."

Nothing.

"I sold a kidney on the internet."

Still nothing.

I snap my fingers under her nose.

She jumps, almost knocking my laptop off my desk. "What?"

I rotate my laptop so she can see the screen. "A dog bakery is not a bad idea. We will make a decent living if we market it correctly. Now, we need to find a place to live that we can afford."

She shakes her thoughts away. "Right. I suggest an apartment at first because we won't have enough money to start a business and put a down payment on a house."

"Good thinking."

Harper shrieks from across the classroom. "I am *not* living in your parents' basement. Not going to happen. You are such a loser."

Dylan replies, "I'd rather be hated for who I am—"

Harper throws her hand up in his face. "If that's another Kurt Cobain quote, I will smack you into tomorrow."

Dylan slings his hair out of his eyes as a wide grin covers his face. "You are a closet Nirvana fan. Admit it."

She flicks his nose. "Don't mess with me."

Kenzie shakes her head. "They have an even worse set of career choices than we do. I guess a mechanic and a teacher won't make much money."

"He should have stayed in school." I tap the laptop again with my pen. "So, apartments. I'm thinking something near Twelve South. It's trendy and near lots of shops. I'll research how much rent would be for a shop with an apartment on top."

She blinks at me. "Uh, that's actually a pretty smart idea."

I lean back and lace my fingers behind my head, my biceps flexing. "I'm a pretty good businessman. You teach me how to bake, and I'll teach you how to run a business. Dad taught me the fine art of pinching pennies."

She jots down some notes then looks over at Michael and Mollie. I turn to see the cute couple. Michael nods while Mollie makes grand gestures with her hands, her face shining bright. It appears their partnership is going well.

Kenzie nods. "Chores. What do you like to do? Or better yet, what do you hate to do?"

"Nobody likes any chores. Why don't we just wing it?"

She shakes her head. "Not a good idea. Unless I know you're going to do the dishes, if I see a pile in the sink, I'll get mad about them and eventually toss them into the dishwasher and bitch about having to do it all the time, and next, I'll throw a dish at you, causing you to call the police, then you'll move out and start dating someone half your age."

I stare at her, knowing exactly where that's coming from. Hamilton mentioned the "dishes" episode about a year ago, and it didn't sound pretty at all. "Wow, you did that without even coming up for air. Any buried hostilities you want to talk about?"

"Nope. Do you want to do the dishes, or do you want to vacuum?"

I think back to when her parents' relationship started to go south. One time I saw blue lights in front of their house, but I never dared ask Kenzie or Michael what that was about.

"How about this? You split up the chores into different categories. I'll do my laundry, and you do your own. We'll do the shopping together. You cook, and I'll clean. And all the yucky stuff that doesn't have to be done every day can be in another category. One week, I do those chores, and the other week, you do them. How does that sound?"

She nibbles on the inside of her cheek. "Sounds like a reasonable plan." Kenzie completes the chore list. "What about yard work?"

"We won't have any since we'll live above our shop, but if we have potted plants, you plant, and I'll water. Deal?"

"You're making it sound easier than it really is."

I shrug. "Some relationships are easy. My mom..." My voice trails off as I think about Mom and Dad. They worked together so well. They enjoyed each other's company, and even though they had their tussles, they never stayed angry for long. "She was one of a kind."

Kenzie places her hand over mine and squeezes it. With a weak smile, she says, "Yes, she was. I miss her."

I clear my throat and pull myself together before I lose it in front of the entire class. "Me too. What's next? If we work ahead, you can be free of me sooner."

She gets a wicked smile on her face. "Great minds think alike."

Damn. I was hoping she would deny her desire to get rid of me. But to avoid showing how disappointed I am, I say, "I knew that would get your attention."

Kenzie sits up tall and throws her shoulders back. "And I have some ideas for your website."

"You're motivated to get away from me, aren't you?"

Kenzie nods. "Definitely. It was *your* idea."

Under my breath, I reply, "Thanks."

She scans the sheet and taps one of the items. "Personal grooming. Not that I spend a ton of money on makeup and stuff like that, but I'm not going without. How much do you need in that department?"

I tap my chin with a finger. "I'm high maintenance. It takes a lot to look this good."

"You seriously need to reevaluate your definition of 'good.'" She looks over at Eli. "That's good, and I don't care if he's only a park ranger. That boy is a hot slice of pizza." She slaps a hand over her mouth. "I can't believe I said that out loud."

Charlie and Eli sit back in their seats with their feet on their desks, apparently very happy with their drama-free fake relationship.

"We've been married ten minutes, and you're already ready to turn me in for a newer model."

"Sorry, but you know I was ready to send you packing before our arrangement."

I lean in close to her. She opened this conversation, so now it's time for me to explore what happened. "Why is that? What did I do to you?"

She buries her head in the paperwork and continues to scribble figures on the worksheet. "You wouldn't understand." Kenzie clears her throat then continues. "Since you don't smoke and you better not take up that habit, I can put zero dollars in that category, right? How much money do you spend each month on video games and movies?"

"A movie sounds like a good idea. Want to go to one on Friday?"

She buries her head farther, and her hair falls over her face like a brunette waterfall. "I can't. Busy that night."

"Saturday?"

"I have a very full social calendar. Sorry."

I blow out a large breath. "Okay. I see where this is going. I'll see you tonight since I'll be at your house anyway for band practice."

She rolls her eyes. "Again? Please tell me Dylan didn't pick out the next set because another week of depressing Nirvana songs is more than I can handle."

"You could join the band, then you'd have a vote on the songs we rehearse."

She shakes her head. "No thanks."

He does a drum riff on my desk. "Come on. You know you're way better on drums than Rhett."

She grins. "True, but I'll stick to fangirling from afar. Anyway, how does this have anything to do with the project?"

"After rehearsal, you're going to teach me how to make bread."

She snaps her head back. "No, I'm not."

I lean back in my seat and cross my arms over my chest. "It's important to the business. You have to teach me. You don't want our family business to fail, do you?"

She groans. "You're taking this all too literally, but fine, I'll teach you how to make bread. I think Mom has a date tonight anyway." Kenzie does a full-body shiver. "If I bake, you have to clean."

I hold out my hand for her to shake. "Deal, Mrs. Shaw."

She takes my hand, and I love how mine devours hers whole. I lock eyes with her.

For a moment, I think I'm going to get away with it, but then she raises her eyebrows. "Stop calling me that, *Aiden*."

Before she can snatch her hand away, I kiss her knuckles.

Tiffany clears her throat. "No PDA in the classroom."

Kenzie and I stare at each other before she scoots away, sensing my next move.

"I'll show you PDA."

Kenzie hides her face with the paper. "Don't do it."

I snatch the paper from her hands and let it drift to the floor while I hover over her desk, our faces only inches away from each other. Kenzie's eyes twinkle with amusement.

"Do what? This?" I grab her hand and lick it, making her squeal.

Hamilton throws a wadded-up piece of paper at me. "Get a room."

Tiffany and Harper look like they swallowed sour pickles. I'm going to take whatever chance I can get to make Kenzie lighten up around me. If they don't like it, they can kiss my butt.

Chapter 13

Thanks to my noise-canceling headphones, I don't hear even one horrible note from the band in the garage. The soothing sounds of Mumford & Sons beat anything Nash Trash could ever make. I love my brother, but he's put together an interesting set of misfits for his garage band. David's bass thumps through the house as Rhett bangs on the hi-hat cymbals way too much. No wonder Mom likes to have date night on Wednesdays. She's out with Collin, which is a yucky combination of browns surrounded by a decent blue, so he's not to be trusted. But Mom wouldn't understand how I already know it's doomed to fail. If she would only listen to me, she would realize she needs to get back with Dad.

I flip through Mom's recipe box and pull out my favorite: sourdough bread. At some point, I should rewrite the recipe on a new index card because this one is crumpled and even has a splatter of dried dough on the corner. Maybe that's why I don't throw it away. Every time I pull it out, I'm reminded of the first time I made the recipe on my own, a time when all four of us were still a happy family. I shake the memory out of my head, retrieve the ingredients needed to make the bread, and line everything up on the counter. Right when I retrieve my rolling pin from the drawer, someone removes my headphones.

I swing around, and the rolling pin misses David's face by an inch as he ducks just in time.

"Watch it, Betty Crocker."

"You scared the crap out of me. Don't you know you shouldn't sneak up on the chef?"

"I do now." He scans the kitchen and all the supplies I have lined up. "You ready to teach me your magic baking skills?"

"If I must. Go wash your hands. No telling what's on that guitar you've been playing."

He bows. "Yes, ma'am, Mrs. Shaw."

I point the rolling pin at his head. "Stop calling me that."

He washes then dries off his hands and walks over to me, holding them out like he's ready to perform surgery. "Teach me the ways."

"We are going to make sourdough bread." I point to a bowl I brought out of the refrigerator. "This is the starter."

His eyebrows scrunch together. "The what?"

I giggle. "It's a base that stays dormant in the refrigerator until you're ready to make bread." I open the lid, take a whiff of it, and moan. "Smell it. It's heavenly."

He leans in, and his eyes get big. "That's good."

"Yeah. We'll add a little of the starter along with the other ingredients, and before long, we'll have some bread. Well, it does take a few hours."

"A few hours?"

"It has to rest. You'll see."

"If you say so."

I let him measure out the ingredients, and he's surprisingly skilled at measuring the portions correctly. I guess since he's had to fend for himself for the last five years, he's had to learn his way around the kitchen.

"Now, dig in with your hands, and mix it. It's the only way to make this work."

He dives in, and the gloppy, sticky dough covers his hands. The muscles in his forearms flex every time he squeezes the dough.

"Take your dough and drop it onto the wax paper."

He drops the dough with a splat then holds up his dough-covered fingers. "How do I get this off?"

I sprinkle his hands with a little flour. "Most of it should come off. Just add it to the pile on the counter."

"Now what do we do?"

I sprinkle some more flour on his dough pile, then I give him an evil grin. "Now for the fun part. I *need* you to *knead* the flour. Get it? I *need* you to *knead* the dough."

"A little baking humor?"

"Yeah. Here's how to do it." I turn on a timer before I nudge him out of the way to douse my hands with flour. With the heels of my hands, I press down into the dough then fold the blob over. Press down and fold, over and over. "See? Can you do that?"

Before I can move out of his way, he sidles up right behind me, his hands over mine as he helps me knead the dough. His breath on my neck sends a shiver down my spine.

"Why don't I move so you can do this easier?"

"I think I need my tutor nearby in case I mess up. Get it. *Knead* my tutor."

"You'll have to do this for eight minutes."

His laughter rumbles in my ear. "Even better. Help me out."

Someone better help *me* out because, even though I've built up a wall to protect myself from all the ugliness his name provides, I'm having a hard time staying strong. I know my system is accurate and he will fail me at some point, but holy fricking cow, his every touch sends a soft, tingly sensation up my arms, and I can even *see* his scent. It's a combination of light green and pink, and it's very pretty.

No! Nothing about him is supposed to be pretty.

His strong arms brush against mine as his hands work the dough, and I don't ever want eight minutes to end. A dusting of flour lingers on his forearms and lands on the faint hairs. I've never noticed the veins on his hands before, but they bulge with each movement.

"If I knew how much fun making bread with my wife would be, I would have asked you to marry me a long time ago."

I turn to face him. Bad idea. He rests his hands on my lower back and moves me up against him. Desire in his eyes, he stares down at me. My hands find his chest, and right as I slide them up to his neck, the timer goes off, making me jump away from him.

"Let's put the dough in a bowl to rest for an hour."

He clears his throat. "An hour then we get to do this again?"

I shake my head. "No, thank goodness."

He chuckles as he washes his hands at the sink while I open the freezer door to cool off my hormones. Someone lets out a wolf whistle behind me. I slam the freezer door and swing around to find Michael, Rhett, and Dylan standing in the kitchen.

Michael points at me. "Looks like you've got a little flour on your backside."

I do my best to twist around to see what he's talking about when Rhett takes a picture. He shows me his phone, and I gasp. Two perfectly shaped floury handprints cover my butt.

I reach for the phone and say, "Delete that now, or I will."

"Okay," he says as he deletes the picture. "Buzzkill."

I swat David in the stomach to stifle his laugh as I storm off toward my room in utter embarrassment. The baking lesson is over for today. I will finish the steps on my own. My face feels like I have a sunburn, and my heart rate is stuck in overdrive. Tonight, I'm going to do a mock-up for David's website so I can be rid of him for good. I don't think I can handle any more one-on-one time with him. He messes with my system, and I can't trust my feelings. Besides, I don't have to because my colors never let me down.

Chapter 14

One step forward and two frickin' giant leaps back. Kenzie was warming up to me, then the guys had to come in and mess things up. Sometimes, my best friends can be jerks. We pile back into the garage and run through two songs, but even Dylan, the most serious of the band, can't stop laughing enough to practice. I thump away on the bass, hoping to break a string, but no one else plays along with me. A swirl of dark maroon and black flashes through my mind. I hate when that happens.

"What are you guys looking at?"

Rhett points with his drumstick to his head. "You've got flour in your hair."

I run a hand through it, and the white powder filters through the air. "Jealous much? I can't blame you. If Tiff were my partner, I'd need some humor in my life too."

Rhett flings a drumstick in my direction. I duck in time for it to sail right over my head.

"How did you ever date that whore of Babylon? The only good thing is that she's such a control freak, she's doing most of the project on her own because she doesn't trust me to do it right, which is fine by me."

With gritted teeth, I reply, "It. Was. One. Date."

Dylan removes his guitar from around his neck and checks his watch. "Which reminds me. Gotta go meet the ole ball and chain my-self. Pray for me."

Hamilton puts a hand on Dylan's head like he's blessing him. "Go in peace, my friend. God be with you."

Dylan bows. "And also with you."

From the way Dylan dresses, it's hard to believe his mother is a Methodist minister and also one of the coolest people on earth. She helped me and Fiona a ton when Mom died. She never tried to sugarcoat the situation. In one of my sessions with her, I yelled, "It's not fair!" She told me that shit happens, and it sucks, and I had a right to feel that way. After that, I allowed myself to be mad at the situation and not at my mother for leaving.

Mollie tiptoes into the garage. Her doe eyes are full of wonder when she stares at Hamilton. He busies himself with the knobs on his keyboard as if doing the most important thing in the world. I wish the two of them would stop this shy game they are playing and admit they like each other.

"Hey, Michael."

He looks up and flashes her a quick smile. "Hey, Molls. What's up?"

"I was looking for Kenzie and thought she might be out here."

Sure, she was. The last place to look for Kenzie would be in the garage, where I am. Mollie knows it, and we all know it's a pathetic excuse to see Michael.

"Oh. She's probably in her room, getting the flour off her butt."

"Huh?"

I hold up a hand. "Don't ask."

"Thanks." She takes a step backward, still watching Hamilton fiddle with his keyboard. "We should finish that form tonight."

"Yeah. We'll be done in here soon."

She grins and gives him a thumbs-up. "Excellent. See you in a bit."

Well, that wasn't subtle.

Rhett chuckles. "Somebody's whipped already."

"Shut up. Like you're any better. At least my fake wife has a real job."

Rhett gasps. "Don't be talking about my world-famous novelist wife." He points a drumstick at Hamilton. "You're just mad that you're unemployed."

Hamilton slams his hands on the keys, setting off a god-awful noise through the garage.

Dylan cringes. "This project is turning all of us into old married men. I draw the line if I start losing hair like my dad."

On instinct, I scratch my head.

"While you guys are trying to one-up each other with your fake wives, I'm going to do some baking with mine."

Hamilton chuckles. "Where will the flour land this time?"

I flip him a bird and saunter back into the kitchen to find Kenzie pounding the ball of dough while Mollie sits on a barstool, flinching every time Kenzie smacks the gooey mess. A cloud of flour filters through the room as she wipes the sweat from her brow with her forearm. She mumbles to herself, and I probably don't want to know what she's saying. Mollie wears a scared expression as if she's afraid to ask what's going on.

"You started the next step without me?"

She jerks up and hits her head on the cabinets above her. "Crap." She turns her attention back to the dough. "It was a quick step, and you were busy, so I pounded it down again. It rests for another hour."

Mollie points to the garage door. "If y'all are done, I'm going to get Michael." Her feet have never moved so fast.

I nod and motion toward the sink. "Can I do the dishes while we wait?"

"Uh... sure, but you don't have to stick around."

"And not eat any of my very first loaf of bread? You're twisted."

She cleans off the counter and hands me the rolling pin. "Have at it, Aiden."

When I reply with a line from her favorite movie, she smacks me with the dishtowel. "Don't quote *The Princess Bride*. It's off-limits to you."

"What about—"

"Stop."

I fill up the sink with sudsy water and scrub the dishes, feeling her eyes on me the entire time.

"How much time do we have left?" I dry off my hands and toss the dishtowel back to her.

She scoots up to sit on the counter and checks her watch. "Another forty-five minutes."

"Good. I'll be back."

As I turn to leave, she says, "You don't have to come back."

"I wouldn't want you to eat all that bread yourself."

"Ugh!"

FIONA AND I STARE EACH other down in our battle of wills. The first one to grin has to do dishes for a week, and I'm tired of losing to my little sister.

With a straight face, she says, "I once held the door open for a clown."

I nod. "Oh yeah?"

"Yep. It was a nice jester."

I shake my head. "I used to be addicted to soap, but I'm clean now."

She rolls her eyes. "Did you hear they found an insect on the moon? They're calling it a lunar tick."

My mouth starts to quiver, and Fiona leans over the table. "Is that a grin?"

I bite the inside of my cheek. "Not even close. I'm terrified of elevators. I'll be taking steps to avoid it."

She squeezes her eyes closed. "Not gonna laugh."

Dad walks into the room. "Hey, guys. I swallowed some food coloring. I think I dyed inside."

Fiona and I crack up at the same time while Dad prances around the kitchen like a proud peacock. "I'm still the king of bad dad jokes, and you two have to do the dishes again."

She crosses her arms over her chest and huffs. "Dad, I was so close to making David crack. I could see it in that twitchy mouth of his." She leans over to give my cheek a pinch.

I lurch over and grab her, throwing her over my shoulder like a sack of potatoes.

She yells, "Let me down!"

I pinch behind her knee, making her squirm even more. "Not until you admit you laughed first."

"Nope."

I tickle her more.

"Put her down, and clean this kitchen." Dad lets out a yawn. "I'm beat." He looks at my pants as his eyebrows rise. "What happened to you?"

I lower Fiona to the floor and twist around to stare at the flour handprints as Fiona giggles. "Nothing. I'm a baker for my class project, and Kenzie was giving me a lesson."

Fiona smacks my butt, and flour dust drifts through the room. "I bet she schooled you."

I smirk at her just as the kitchen timer buzzes.

"Time for the next step of the bread. See ya," I say as I head to the door.

"Can I come?" Fiona rushes to the door.

"No."

"Take your sister."

Fiona smiles, and her smirk says, "Nana-nana boo-boo."

I growl at her, but it's all in jest. I lean down, and Fiona jumps on my back.

"See ya later, Dad."

He leans against the doorframe and throws one more dad joke our way. "Did you know without nipples, boobs would be pointless?"

Heat rises over my neck, and I make it halfway across the road before I bust out a laugh.

From our front porch, he says, "You lose."

After Fiona knocks on the Hamiltons' door, Kenzie blinks a few times. "Oh my."

I let Fiona slide off my back, and she wraps her arms around Kenzie. "Hey, Zee."

"You have gotten so much taller. Pretty soon, I'll have to look up to you."

Fiona giggles when she sees the back of Kenzie's jeans.

"Fi, what are you doing?"

She shrugs. "Just checking to see if she has handprints on her butt too."

Kenzie gasps and stares at me like I'm supposed to control what comes out of this kid's mouth. "Uh, what are you doing here?"

I rub my hands together. "The bread. It's time for the next step."

"Oh. I didn't know you were coming back. I just threw it in the oven."

Fiona inhales and runs into the kitchen. "Can I see?"

Before she can open the oven door, Kenzie reaches her and puts an arm out, preventing her from doing anything. "Can't do that. It will make the bread fall."

All defeated, Fiona frowns. "Oh. How long?"

Kenzie looks at her watch. "About twenty minutes."

Fiona's frown turns into a smile. "Yay. We can play the bad-dad-joke game until it's ready."

Kenzie's brow crinkles, and she bites her lip.

"Fiona, why don't you draw Kenzie a picture? Show how good you're getting."

"Dogs are my favorite to draw. Want to see?"

She's going to flip when Dad brings home a puppy for her. It's about to kill me to keep the secret.

Kenzie blinks and nods. "Sure." She rifles through a drawer and pulls out a notepad and pencil.

While Fiona buries her face in the paper, I sneak a peek at Kenzie. She flicks her eyes from Fiona to me then the oven, then back to me. She glances away, her fingers wringing a dish towel.

"Smells good."

Kenzie takes a deep inhale. "I love that aroma."

"Me too."

Fiona lifts her face and takes a deep breath. "Yeah. Your house smells better than ours does. Ours smells like dude feet and farts."

Kenzie presses her lips into a thin line while I try to find a hole to bury my entire body in.

"Well, it's true. You and Dad are gross." She turns back to Kenzie. "Your dad and brother must not fart because it smells good over here."

Someone kill me now. "Fi…"

"It's okay. All dads fart. I have special ways of masking the odor." She waves her hand toward the oven. "Works every time."

Fiona stares up at me. "We need to bake more often."

Thank God the oven timer goes off because it could not get any more uncomfortable. Fiona jumps out of her chair and lunges for the oven door.

"Fi, let Kenzie get that. It's really hot."

Fiona sticks her tongue out at me but steps out of the way to let Kenzie manage oven duty. When Kenzie removes the two loaves from the oven and places them on a cooling rack, my jaw drops. They are perfect.

I point to them. "I did that?"

Kenzie gives me a warning look. "*We* did that."

My mouth waters. I've never been so proud of such a simple act in all my life. I go to touch one loaf, and Kenzie pops my hand.

"Ow."

"Too hot. Patience, Mr. Shaw. You don't know much about baking, do you? Too hot and you'll get burned. Wait too long, and it's cold and hard."

Kind of like you?

She must be a mind reader, because she steels her eyes on me as she snatches a bread knife out of the storage block. She points it at me, and my hands immediately fly up in surrender.

"Want to do the honors?"

"Yes, ma'am, Mrs. Shaw."

Fiona giggles as she hops off the barstool she was perching on.

I puff out my chest when I take control of the knife. "Let me show you how it's done."

Fiona and Kenzie groan. When I slice into the crispy crust, steam rises. The soft center is moist but not doughy, and I can't believe it turned out so nicely. I slice all of one loaf, and Kenzie retrieves a tub of butter and a jar of jam. The three of us scarf down one loaf without saying a word other than our moans of utter satisfaction.

Kenzie smiles at me and points to her chin. "You got a little jam on your chin."

My tongue snakes out to clean up the residual but can't find it. After I wipe my mouth with a napkin, I sit back and pat my stomach. "Kenz, that was awesome."

She peers down the hallway toward the garage. "We better hide this other loaf before the rest of Nash Trash scarfs it down."

I point to my mouth. "You can hide it right here. Besides, the only ones left are Hamilton and Mollie. I doubt they even know we exist right now."

She slides the loaf into a paper bag and hands it to Fiona. "Take this to your dad, and get out of here before Michael comes in and steals it from you."

Fiona snatches the bag and pulls Kenzie down to her level to kiss her on the cheek before she darts toward the door. "Thanks, Zee."

She races across the street, and I keep an eye on her until she's safely inside.

Then I turn to face Kenzie. "I'm so sorry about—"

She puts up a hand to stop me. "It's okay. She didn't mean anything by it."

"I know, but…"

Kenzie straightens up the kitchen, anything to avoid the dad conversation. "This was fun. I'll research some dog treat recipes for next time."

"Don't tell Fi, but we might have a little taste tester at the Shaw house soon."

She covers her mouth and sucks in a breath. "She's going to be so surprised."

"Yep, soon, our house will smell like male farts and dog poop."

She wipes down the counter then hands me dishes to put in the cupboard. "It will be worth it to make her happy. She deserves it. And I'm sure the dog won't be very picky about our treats."

"Good for our egos, don't you think?"

"I guess."

Hamilton and Mollie barrel through the door toward us, their noses like those of bloodhounds.

Hamilton searches the oven. "Where's the bread?"

Kenzie and I share a glance, then I say, "Well, it didn't turn out so well. I had to throw it away in the outside garbage can."

His shoulders slump. "Dang. It smelled so good."

Kenzie pats his back. "Maybe next time."

I jerk a thumb toward the door. "I better go. See you tomorrow, wifey-poo?"

She smacks me on the arm as she leads me to the door. "Get used to sleeping on the couch."

"Oooooh, burn," Mollie says.

"Night, Kenzie, and about Fi. Thanks for overlooking..."

"Fiona is sweet and would never mean any harm. I, uh..." Her eyes flick up to meet mine. "I miss her."

I wave and walk backward until I reach the street. She closes the door, but when I get to my front door, I turn around and catch her peeking out the window, watching me. Maybe I caught her in between being too hot and too cold. But if I'm being honest with myself, she's always just right for me.

Chapter 15

David, otherwise known as Aiden to me, better appreciate the work I'm putting into this website for him. I spent four hours searching for the perfect WordPress theme, Marchato, because it's pretty. If I'm going to spend time staring at the screen, I might as well see something pleasing. The deep-purple *M* and the medium-blue *C* are very lovely together.

Using a few band photos Michael posted on Instagram, I insert some cool shots of each member, and as placeholders, I add the stupidest stuff I could think of for the band member bios. Michael's was the easiest, and he'll kick my butt when he finds out I mentioned he used to lip-sync to Boy George. Of course, I used Kurt Cobain quotes for Dylan. But for David, I used an old school picture, the one when he was about seven when he insisted on wearing his Batman costume for picture day.

I giggle thinking about it. David was so proud, and unlike my mother, who would have had a hissy fit, his mother walked him into the classroom and gave him a high five. God, I miss her.

Michael taps on my door. "I gotta go. Mollie's got me shopping for apartments."

I scrub my face with my hands and yawn. "Is it really nine o'clock in the morning already?"

"What are you doing?" he asks.

Stretching my arms over my shoulders, I reply, "Working on David's website."

He peeks over my shoulder, but I block his view with my notebook of sketches for the site. "No peeking."

"You stayed up all night working on that?"

"Yep. The faster I finish, the sooner I'm done with the school project."

Michael groans. "It's not that bad, is it? You should be ashamed of letting him do all the work."

I hold my hands out in front of me in defense. "Hey, it was his idea."

He rolls his eyes. "How close are you to being done with it?"

"Not close enough, but I've got the framework done." I close out of the website and stand. Another yawn escapes my mouth. "I need to shower before my ugly husband comes knocking on the door to check out bakeries today."

"Woof."

I throw a wadded-up piece of paper at him. "Shut up, you unemployed sorry excuse for a husband. Living off your nurse wife's salary. You should be ashamed of yourself."

He chuckles. "Living the dream."

"Get out of here."

Michael ducks to miss the paper then runs down the hallway. Now to get this lack-of-sleep funk off me. With the framework for the website done, I should be free of David within a few days. That is if he stands by his end of the deal. Just in case, I researched some areas where we could open up a dog bakery. The more I googled, the more interesting it became. There are seven dog parks in the Nashville area and not one doggie bakery within walking distance of even one of them. Coincidentally, there is a vacant building across from Edwin Warner Park that would be perfect, and it's not in the high-rent district of town, so we might be able to afford it.

Muffled voices from down the hall wake me up better than a large cup of coffee from Bongo Java. I scoot toward the bathroom when I hear David's deep rumbly chuckle come from behind me.

"Nice PJs."

Of course he would catch me in my Hello Kitty boy shorts. I swing around to see him leaning against the wall, chewing on a bagel I'm sure my mother offered him. "One day, I'm going to catch you wearing your old Ninja Turtles footie pajamas."

He throws his head back and lets out a huge belly laugh. "Kenz, you shouldn't make promises you don't intend to keep."

"Aiden... what are you doing here so early?"

David stalks toward me. "If you must know, Mrs. Shaw, I couldn't wait to make a big dent in this project today."

Right when he is within punching distance, I take a step backward toward the bathroom. "You'll have to wait a few more minutes. I have morning breath and bed head." I point to my rat's nest on top of my head.

His mouth twitches as he takes another step in my direction. "I don't see a problem." He sniffs my breath, making me gasp. "I don't smell a problem either."

I push away from him. "No matter what you think, I need a shower. You..." I point behind him. "Go find something to keep you busy while I shower." I snap my fingers. "Come with me." He follows me like a puppy to my room. I nudge him into my desk chair and then lean over him to open up my laptop again, and I'm certain he took another sniff of me. I'm pretty sure Tiffany smells like lilacs after farting, so maybe my funk will turn him off. "I stayed up all night working on your website. It's not done, but it will give you an idea of where I'm going with it."

His big hand latches on to mine as I try to walk away. "Walk me through this."

"You're not helpless." I point to the menu items. "Up top you have the main sections I thought would be most important, but I can change them."

He nods as he recites, "About us, inspirations, tour dates, merch... Kenz, this is looking good." David peers up at me. "I could never have done this on my own."

I shrug. "I'm not done, but within a few days, I'll be able to hand it over to you."

He stares up at me. "You're something else."

I wag my finger in front of his nose. "Not really. Remember our deal."

Before I can back away, he tickles my side. "My wife won't let me forget it."

"Keep clicking around and jot down some areas you want changed, and I'll be back soon."

David's eyes feel like they are trained on me as I rush out of my room. I turn on the shower, and before I dive into the steamy water, I hear David's rumbly laughter again.

A knock to the bathroom door scares a squeak out of me. "What?"

"Batman?"

I was wondering how long it would be before he clicked on his bio. "Yeah, well, that was all I had at the time. I think it's a good look for you."

"You would. I think you can do better than that."

"Can't hear you. Gotta jump in the shower before I run out of hot water."

I lunge into the shower and jerk the curtain closed behind me. Sorry, not sorry. I wish I could have seen the look in his eyes when he ran across that picture. But knowing David, I may have just started a pissing match with him. No telling what he'll put in our project from our past. I clearly didn't think this one all the way through.

He wouldn't dare add the picture of me playing outside with him and Michael, all three of us without shirts. We were so young, but if he still has a copy of it, I'm doomed. I hope he wouldn't jeopardize our project just to get back at me. At least I don't think he would. I'd better play nice, or this could really backfire.

Chapter 16

If I didn't think I'd scare her away, I'd get her back for using my Batman school photo as my bio picture. But the more I poke around on what she's done so far, the more I'm convinced I've got the right person helping me. It looks great, and with only a few minor changes it should be ready to submit to Bellevue sooner than I anticipated. That's awesome because I want to check that off my to-do list, but then again, it means I lose my partner in crime for our school project. This was my idea, but I was hoping it would take her weeks to finish. I definitely underestimated Kenzie's talents—or her desire to get rid of me.

Her peach scent hits me before she even makes it near her bedroom door. I didn't mind her just-rolled-out-of-bed appearance, but I'm not going to complain about the way she smells right now. When she enters, piling her hair on the top of her head, I almost fall out of my chair. Her bra strap peeks out of her tank top, and her jeans leave nothing to the imagination. Even though they are grungy, they fit perfectly on her.

"What?"

I blink away my stare. "Uh, you clean up good."

She smacks me on the arm as expected then hums the tune to Batman.

"You are so funny. I texted you a picture of me with my bass so you can update the photo now to something more appropriate."

Kenzie leans down to tie her sneakers, giving me a quick flash of cleavage. "What I picked out *is* appropriate. In fact, I think you should add that theme song to your playlist."

I snatch a sneaker out of her hand and hold it up out of her reach. "Do you want me to add to our project that you like to role-play the sword fight from *The Princess Bride* every night before bed?"

She gasps. "You wouldn't."

"I would. In fact, I might have already done that."

She steels her eyes at me before she snatches her shoe out of my hand, grabs her purse and a canvas bag, and marches toward the hall. "Let's get this day done before I get the six-fingered man after you."

"No match for the Dread Pirate Roberts, and you know it." I wave my hand in front of me. "After you, Mrs. Shaw."

When she passes me, she pops me in the stomach. Kenzie's mom sits at the kitchen table, texting on the phone, and by the growl that Kenzie lets out, I'm assuming her mother is having a conversation with the latest boyfriend.

"Bye, Mom. We have school stuff to work on."

"Will you be home tonight? Collin's going to take us out to dinner."

"Not hungry."

Kenzie bounds out of the house. Her mother's mouth gapes open. Mrs. Hamilton turns to me, and I shrug and say, "I'll get her home in plenty of time and make sure she's hungry."

Her weak smile lets me know she appreciates my attempt to be the middle man, but it will be futile. "Thanks, David. I'm glad you two are hanging out again."

"Me too. I'll see you later."

Kenzie is halfway across the road before I can even close her front door. When she gets to my car, she paces back and forth in front of it.

"You okay?"

"Nope. Let's go."

She slams the passenger door closed so hard I think she bent the metal frame.

"Do you want to—"

"No. Just drive."

"Yes ma'am, Mrs. Shaw."

She chews on her bottom lip, and if I look closely, I might see steam spewing from her ears. When I get to the end of our street, she points toward the right. "Go toward Edwin Warner Park. There's something I want you to see."

"As you wish."

"If you don't stop, I'm going to quote my favorite movie."

"Touché. By the way, you smell very nice. Way better than morning breath."

She stares out the window and taps her fingers on the armrest to the Portugal. The Man song I have blaring out of my speakers. Without asking for permission, I pull into the Donut Den for a quick morning coffee-and-donut run. "I'll be right back." She pulls out the wallet from her purse, but I wave her off. "I've got this."

"It's not a date."

"Sweetheart, I don't take dates to the Den. I have way more class than that."

She hands me a five-dollar bill. "Exactly. So as long as it's not a date, I'll pay for my own."

I snatch it out of her hand and growl. "Fine." What she doesn't know is that I'll hide it in her purse when she's not looking.

While I stand in line at the Den, Tiffany walks up behind me. I do my best to pretend I don't see her, but it's impossible with her obnoxious perfume wafting around me.

"Hey, cutie."

My stomach lurches when I hear her nails-on-a-chalkboard voice. She's always looming around corners, ready to pounce.

"What's up?" I don't even turn around. I train my eyes on the donut selection even though I already know what I'm buying.

"I'm meeting Rhett to go to some open houses. You see, with his salary, we can afford to live in Belle Meade."

"Have fun with those property taxes."

She giggles a bit too loudly for my taste. "At least *my* spouse is loaded, plus he's hot, unlike yours which is a complete basket case."

I point out each item I want from the display case, and while Reggie fills two cups of coffee, I do my best to ignore the lame insults she lobs my way about Kenzie. I hold the bag of donuts under my arm as I grab both cups of coffee.

"Have fun with that nutjob Kenzie today. You know she hates your guts." The twinkle in her eye shows she knows she's got me right where she wants me.

"You're probably right, but a little bit of bling does wonders for someone's attitude."

Tiffany's mouth drops open, making me certain my words hit the intended target.

"See ya."

She scans the store, and when she spies Kenzie in my car, she gets a wicked grin on her face. Before I can react, Tif grabs my face and plants a big kiss on my lips. I try to back away, but with a bag of donuts under my arm and a cup of scalding hot coffee in each hand, I'm pretty much stuck. I lurch backward as I pry my face off of hers.

"What the...?"

"Have fun today."

She pushes past me to give Reggie her order. When I get the courage to glance at Kenzie, all she can muster up is a head wag.

I hand her one coffee cup and the bag of donuts before I rush around to get into the driver's seat. "Kenzie, she's a leech. She ambushed me."

"I know. It doesn't matter."

I let out a sigh. "It matters to me and not just because of this project. Because you are my friend. I don't like Tiffany. At all."

"I said it doesn't matter. Jeez."

"Oookay."

She stares out the window as I drive away toward Edwin Warner Park. When she points to a vacant parking spot, I pull in then turn off my car. In silence, we eat our donuts and drink coffee. She dusts off the cinnamon powder from her hands then exits my car. "Come on. I want to show you something."

I follow her across the street to an old building that's for sale. She stands in front of it and stares up at the structure. "I think this would be the perfect spot for the Barkery." She points to the upstairs. "There's a small studio apartment up there, and it's right across from the most popular dog park in town." She chuckles. "I'm surprised someone hasn't had this idea before in real life."

I nod. "It's perfect. And we could have dog water bowls out on the sidewalk and some benches for the owners to hang out."

She bounces up and down. "I have another idea. We could get some of those oversize tricycles, and we can ride them handing out treats throughout the park." Her face lights up with enthusiasm.

I fist bump her. "I like it."

She runs back to the car.

"Where are you going?"

"I've got to sketch this while it's all fresh in my head." She runs back with her canvas bag and plops down on the sidewalk. From the bag, she retrieves a notepad and pencil. I plunk down beside her, peering over her shoulder while she draws so fast on the page, it's as if she needs to get it on paper before her vision of the idea fades. I'm the same way with lyrics. Too many times, I've bolted upright in the middle of the night with the perfect line, and if I don't write it down that instant, the idea is gone forever.

"You're really good at this stuff."

She shrugs like it is no big deal. "I don't know. When I get an idea, I have to run with it." She shows me her rough sketch. "What do you think?" Kenzie even drew me standing next to the door with a dog sitting at my feet.

"It's great. Does it fit our budget?"

She cringes. "I saw the listing online, and we'd have to take out a business loan, but we could make it work. I know we could."

We gaze into each other's eyes. She clears her throat. "I mean if this was real, I think it would work." She bows her head, letting a strand of hair that escaped her bun fall over her face as she adjusts her drawing. "I mean, it's not where *Tif* would want to live." She blows out a breath. "You like her, don't you?"

"Kenzie, don't you believe me?"

"I mean, it doesn't matter to me. I was just wondering why. Why are guys so attracted to her, or maybe not her specifically, but girls like her? Just because she's pretty on the outside, which is up for debate in my opinion, she always gets the pick of any guy she wants."

Kenzie stares out over to the dog park, a smidgen of cinnamon powder still rests on her cheek. With my thumb, I swipe it off.

"She's a shiny penny, but eventually people realize that she's not even made of copper. She's just a mixture of a few boring metals, mostly zinc. Not rare and certainly not precious."

Kenzie grins. "Where did that come from?"

"I have no idea, but it was pretty good. You got to admit, right?" *Must write that down.*

She bumps me with her shoulder. "Yes, Aiden, that was a very good analogy."

"Okay, Mrs. Shaw, what's next on our project?"

She rolls her eyes. "The grocery store."

I stand and hold my hands out for her to take, which she does, surprising the crap out of me. After she bounces to a standing position, I say, "Let's do this."

What Kenzie doesn't understand is that she's the most precious of metals and certainly the rarest of all gems. She's one of a kind.

Chapter 17

It seems as if everyone in our class had the same idea because there is no other good reason to be at the grocery store today. Mollie bounces as she walks, talking ninety miles a minute as Michael nods and scratches down notes. David pulls out his grocery list, which contains mostly prepackaged, processed items.

I crinkle my nose. "We can make healthier choices, don't you think?"

He scans his list. "What's wrong with Honey O's cereal?"

"Mainly that there is no honey in it. It's pure cane sugar. We won't have extra money to get a bunch of cavities filled and get your insulin shots daily, so let's do better than that."

I unfold my list and show it to him. He licks his lips as he reads over my shoulder. "Yours is way better, but..." He gets an evil grin on his face. "Does this mean you're going to cook for your man? I could get used to breakfast in bed."

Clearly, I didn't think this one through. "Don't count on it. I'll teach you."

Dylan crashes into the display of Bartlett pears, sending them tumbling onto the floor. "Get me out of here. Harper wants me to eat tofu. I'm a growing boy. I need meat and lots of it. And real cheese. Not gooey soy product pressed into white squares."

The sound of Harper's clickity heels resonates through the produce aisle, announcing her arrival at any minute.

Dylan hides behind me as if I'm large enough to conceal his existence. "She doesn't understand the life of a musician. Everybody knows I eat mac and cheese, the kind out of a box."

I peer at David. "Is this a Kurt Cobain thing?"

He feigns shock. "How did you guess?"

"Well, it's Dylan, and there's no other explanation why someone would choose to eat boxed mac and cheese."

David stares down at me. "We eat it all the time."

If someone poked me with a hot dagger straight in the eye, I think it would hurt less. I point to my chin. "Go ahead. Knock my block off for being so inconsiderate."

He rears back and swings his arm toward me. I squeeze my eyes shut because it looks like he's going to hit me. When nothing happens, I dare to open my eyes. His hand is a hair's breadth from my face.

He winks. "If you think I would really hit you, you don't know me at all."

"I was teasing, but when you reared back, I thought you might be mad enough to smack me."

David shakes his head. "I don't hit girls, no matter how annoying they are."

Tiffany turns the corner with a huge shopping cart, items spilling over the top. In a singsongy voice, she says, "Hello, small-business owners with measly salaries. I'm having fun buying all these organic items because my rich husband and I can afford it."

I lift a gallon jug of water from her cart. "Free-range water? What the heck does that even mean?"

From over my shoulder, Dylan reads the label. "Free-range, gluten-free... water?"

Tiffany snatches the bottle out of my hand. "You don't know anything." She sounds high and mighty, but the flush across her face makes me think she now realizes how stupid her purchase is.

David bumps my shoulder. "I guess us poor small-business owners will never understand the health benefits of free-range water."

"And someday, maybe, if we save our pennies, we can afford cholesterol-free ice."

While David, Dylan, and I get a chuckle at Tiffany's expense, she steels her eyes at me. "You just wait, Kenzie. Your day is coming."

She swivels her cart around and clicks away from us.

Dylan shakes his head. "Dude, I'll take my tofu-eating teacher wife any day over that cray-cray."

They laugh, but I clench my teeth. Making fun of a disability usually makes my skin crawl, but this one hits too close to home—my brain operating as it does. "That is not nice. I'm not on Team Tiffany, but calling someone crazy is so *not* cool."

Dylan throws his hands up in defense. "My bad."

David touches my shoulder. "He didn't mean anything by it, but you've got to admit someone has to have a few screws loose to buy free-range water. If anyone fits the description of 'cray,' it's Tif."

"I'm serious—"

"Oh, Dylan..." Harper's syrupy voice makes Dylan jump a foot off the ground, and he yelps like a little girl. "There you are. Let's go. I have to teach you how to eat healthily."

She grabs his hand, and as she drags him away, he mouths, "Help me."

David and I wave as he begs like he's being led to slaughter.

David tsks. "Poor guy. He and Rhett are so miserable. I think they are starting to go bald."

I stand on my tiptoes to run my hand through his hair and immediately regret it. His eyebrows shoot up so high they get lost in his hairline.

I jerk my hand back like his hair burned it. "I, uh... I was checking to see if I was making you lose your hair."

David slides a hand through a lock of my hair, and I swat him away. He chuckles. "Just making sure I'm not making you bald either."

I push the shopping cart away from the produce section and into the deli section. "Do you like any of these salads?"

"Whatever you want, as long as it's not from a box."

"Burn."

For the next hour, we browse the aisles, looking for the five meals we are to fake-pay for while I continue to steam over Dylan's comment. I know he was trying to be funny, but it's not humorous to say someone has a mental illness. And there's no excuse for David's commentary. The way they fed off one another's insults was terrible, even if it was directed at a horrible person.

Since I shop all the time, I get into the zone and take the lead. David pushes the shopping cart and uses his cell phone as a calculator. His use of the word "cray" still buzzes in my head.

Once we get to the frozen-food section, he lets out a groan.

Maybe he's realized what he said was hurtful. "What's the matter?"

"We just went over our budget."

I snatch his phone out of his hand. "How is that possible? We haven't even gotten to the dairy aisle."

He grabs it back. "We'll have to reevaluate our menu. I know the box items aren't as healthy, but we have to cut corners somewhere."

"There are better ways."

"Like what?"

I shrug. "I don't know. We can eat healthily and still be on a budget."

"It's clear you don't have much experience living on a budget."

"Oh, please." I roll my eyes. "It's not like I'm poor or anything, but we've always had a budget."

He freezes and turns so sluggishly I think he's in slow motion. "Poor?"

His steely stare coupled with his shaky tone for that one word causes me to play back what I said.

Oh, crap. "I didn't mean it like that. I just meant—"

"You meant I am poor and you're not."

David picks up the pace, and I have a hard time keeping up with him.

"That's not what I meant at all."

"You meant every word. Just for your information, there are better things in life than money." He glowers at me. "Like having a family."

I grab the cart from his grip and latch onto his arm. "I know."

"Dad doesn't make a lot of money, but he's always there for me and Fi. Always."

The blood drains from my face with his words and, more importantly, what he's trying to convey. "Wait a second. You think my father doesn't care about me because he's not there anymore?"

David throws his hands up in defense.

I stomp my foot. "My father loves me, and as soon as he realizes how much he misses my mother, he'll be back. You wait and see."

He lets out a deep sigh. "Whatever. Let's just put all this crap back on the shelves and get out of here. I have other things to do."

He's acting like a jerk, but I'm not much better. Whatever. He's being ugly, and I knew he would be this way. It was only a matter of time.

"You're right. Let's get this stuff back on the shelves, then you need to take me home. I've almost done with the website. I'll easily finish it tonight. You'll get what you want, and I'll be done working with you."

"Fine."

"Fine." I don't feel fine. I feel horrible. I feel ugly.

Chapter 18

My knuckles are white from the grip I have on the shopping cart. Kenzie lives in this stupid dream world and is never happy until it's all perfect and orderly. She doesn't care if other people are miserable as long as she's happy. She did me a favor a long time ago when she started giving me the cold shoulder.

Her dig about being poor was low, and it's the first time I've ever heard that insult from her. Kenzie's family having more money than mine must be why she thinks she's so much better than I am. My family's financial situation is out of my control, so if that's her issue with me, then so be it. I can't control that any more than she can control her father leaving.

As much as it pains me, I guess I'm better off not trying to have any type of relationship with her if that's how she sees me. My chest is so tight with frustration, but at the same time, the thought of giving up on any chance with Kenzie carves a deep hole in my heart.

At least Kenzie has the good sense not to say a word as I shove items back on the shelf, not caring if it's the right aisle. I slam the bread down in the soup aisle, and it slides off the shelf onto the floor.

"We have the information we need and can check this section off our 'to-do list' for the project," she says.

"Yeah. One step closer to being done. I'll be out of your hair as soon as you can provide a submission-worthy website." This cannot end soon enough.

"Hey, I don't have to do anything for you."

I storm through the parking lot toward my car, with Kenzie on my heels. "You said you would. Don't back out on me now. I said I'd finish the school project, remember?" I unlock the passenger car door, and she pushes in front of me to get in before I can open it for her. *Whatever.* I slam my hand on the roof of the car before I get in.

We sit in the car, both staring straight ahead.

After a few moments of stewing, she rotates in her seat and sighs. "Can we do a reset because this day started fine? I know I'm a hot mess."

I belt out a laugh. "That's an understatement."

"Hey, I'm trying to apologize." She rests her hand on my thigh.

If there was a way to reset, it's by her hand touching my leg. I already feel the tension leaving my body. I adjust in my seat so her hand falls away. "A simple 'I'm sorry' would be sufficient."

"Those are the two most difficult words for me to say."

I pull out of the parking lot and head toward our homes. "You are a piece of work. I don't get you most of the time."

She stares out her window as we speed down Hillsboro Road. "Yeah, well, get in line. You don't understand."

That's another understatement. I slam my hand on the steering wheel. "What is it that I don't understand? Tell me because I'm not getting it. Do you think you're better than me?"

"No, it's—"

"Because you aren't. You're hot. You're cold. Mean, then nice. I can't keep up with your frickin' roller coaster of emotions." I don't know why I should feel bad about my words, but I do. I run a hand through my hair. "Look, this project is getting to us because we're not used to spending so much time together. We are clearly getting on each other's nerves."

Kenzie draws a slow breath. "I guess."

"I'll work on some of the assignments tonight. You finish my website, and we'll go our separate ways. All you'll have to do is stand next to me during the oral presentation and pretend you helped."

She stares at her fisted hands, and I point to the one with my mother's ring on it. "And as soon as our grades are posted, I expect that back. It stays in *my* family."

Barely over a whisper, she says, "I don't know what to say—"

I slam my fist on the steering wheel, and she jumps. "Why do you hate me so much?" She opens her mouth to answer, but I throw out a hand to stop her. "Never mind. I've learned to get over that." *Liar.* "Why are you such a snob?"

She gasps. "I am not a snob."

"Are too. You talk about how Tif is, but you're no better. At least Tiffany is consistent. You're all over the place."

Her breath hitches, and I already regret my words.

She clears her throat and wipes a tear from her eye. Barely above a whisper, she says, "I should not have said that stuff about your family. I'm... sorry." She lets out a deep breath. "You'll have a fully functioning website by Monday. Then you won't have to deal with my emotions anymore."

My car hits the curb as I jerk it into my driveway. I slam the gear into park. "Sounds good to me."

Without opening the door for her or walking her home or even a simple goodbye, I yank open the car door, jump out, and slam it behind me. I take the steps to my front door two at a time and unlock my house. I don't care what her reason is for hating me. It's not important. I don't even care if she's upset.

Although I do glance out my bedroom window and catch her peeking out of hers. I flop down on my bed, making the mattress bounce as I think back over the morning's events. We were actually getting along, then she had to make that stupid comment about being poor, and I snapped. This project is going to be a disaster, and I wouldn't put it past her to mess up my website so much I'll never get into Bellevue.

Girlish squeals from the living room jolt me out of my funk.

"Thank you, thank you, thank you!" Fiona's voice filters down the hallway.

I force myself off my bed and follow her giggles to the kitchen, where I find Fiona lying on the floor, being smothered in puppy kisses. At least, I think it's a puppy. It has no hair except for a tuft on its head and feet.

"What is that?"

"It's my baby. Isn't she beautiful?"

I cock an eyebrow and peek over to Dad, who beams from ear to ear. He rarely gets to make one of us this happy, so even though I think it's a pretty unusual-looking dog, Fiona is elated, and so is Dad.

"Yes, she is." I kneel beside her and let the dog climb into my lap.

She immediately decides my face needs washing and even slips her tongue into my mouth, making me gag. Fiona giggles.

"You have to keep your mouth closed. She loves to give kisses."

"I see that."

The two of us shower this adorable, hairless critter with hugs and kisses as the dog bounces from my lap to Fiona's.

Dad leans back against the kitchen counter, taking it all in. "So, Fi. You like her?"

"Duh. I love her."

"Now, she won't get much bigger than what she is right now, so that's good."

I scratch under the dog's chin, making her groan with satisfaction. "When will her hair come in?"

Dad chuckles. "She's a Chinese Crested. That's it. All her litter-mates were adopted, and she was so sad all alone. Every time I walked past her cage, I heard her saying to me, 'Please take me to Fiona.'" His voice gets all squeaky, making Fiona giggle.

After she gives another lick to my nose, I plop her back into Fiona's lap. "So, what's her name?"

Fiona chews on her lip and looks down at the hairless pup. "Her name is Cat."

Dad scrunches his brow. "You're going to name a dog Cat?"

Fiona stares at Dad then turns to me. "He is so old."

I belt out a laugh. "Dad, Catarina is a character in *Prince Not-So-Charming*."

He bends down to pick up Catarina, and he's rewarded with a shower of kisses. "Well, Cat, welcome to the Shaw house. Stay off the furniture. You got it?"

The dog licks Dad's nose, and I know that rule will be broken before the night is over.

Dad pulls out a frozen pizza for dinner. "How did your shopping trip go?"

I groan. "At first it was fine, but... I don't want to talk about it."

Fiona laughs as she rubs Cat's belly. "Now you *have* to talk about it."

Here goes nothing. "Dad, do you consider us poor?"

He freezes then turns around and scrubs his face with his hands. "Why do you ask?"

I shrug. "I don't know. Just working on this project has made me think about how hard it is to make ends meet with two incomes. With just one, it's got to be next to impossible."

Dad turns on the oven and tosses the pizza inside. "It is hard, and I'm not going to lie, money is very, very tight."

Tears pool in Fiona's eyes. "Are we going to lose our house?"

He ruffles her hair. "No, sweetie. We will be fine. We just don't have much left over after all the bills are paid every month. But you're right. It's much easier with two incomes."

"You could get married again."

Dad and I stare at Fiona. Her words are so matter-of-fact, like it's a no-brainer. When I get the courage to peek up at Dad, he's lost all the color in his face.

"It's not that simple, Fi. It's more than paying the bills and sharing the chores. Your mom was so special, I…"

His voice trails off, and I need to take over the conversation before we're all in tears and Catarina starts howling. "Fi, do you want to go to the pet store to pick out a bed for Cat?"

And just like that, her thoughts of getting Dad hitched are a faint memory. "Yes. Dad, save us some pizza."

Dad pats me on the back. "You bet. You might want to get her a sweater too. With no hair, she might need one, even in the summer." He slides me some cash then wipes his face with his hands. He'll probably go without lunch for a week to pay for the bed, but he wouldn't have it any other way.

Fiona clips the leash to Cat's collar and bounces toward the door. "Let's go. I can't wait to show her off."

Dad clears his throat. "Hey, Fi. What do you call a fake noodle?"

She shrugs.

"An impasta."

We groan as we head out the door.

When we are far enough away from him, Fi says, "His jokes are getting worse."

And just when I thought my day couldn't get worse, Kenzie stands by the road, retrieving stuff from her mailbox. When Fiona sees Kenzie, Fi gets all wild-eyed and takes off in a jog, Catarina running right alongside her.

"Zee, look what I got!"

Kenzie looks up to see the critter trotting her way, and she backs up a few steps. She stares at me, and I give her the evil eye. Kenzie can get all pissy with me, but Fi is completely off-limits. One snarky comment, and I'll put her in her place.

"Wow! You got a dog?"

"Uh-huh. Today! Daddy brought her home. Isn't Cat pretty?"

Kenzie chews on her lip then grins. "I think Cat is adorable. And such a pretty name."

She leans down to pet the dog, which gives Catarina permission to shower Kenzie with kisses. Kenzie giggles as she attempts to avoid getting a tongue in her mouth.

"Better watch it. You don't know where that mouth has been." I give her my best smirk.

Fiona cackles. "Yeah, because the last person's mouth it was in was his." She jerks her thumb over to me.

Kenzie's eyes get big.

"Fi, we should go."

She picks up the squirmy pup, and between licks to the face, she says, "We're going to the pet store. Wanna come?"

Kenzie shakes her head. "I better not. I promised your brother a rocking website, so I should get to work on it."

I snort. "You know what? I changed my mind. I'll figure it out on my own." I just sealed my fate, but I would rather be up to my neck in student loans than be beholden to her.

Her face falls. "We had a deal."

"Not anymore. See you Monday, Mrs. Shaw."

Kenzie stomps her foot. "Ugh."

Fiona stares at me until I look at her.

"What?"

She rolls her eyes, doing her best preteen impression. "You two need to go to marriage counseling."

I stare at Kenzie, and on cue, we both roll our eyes. Just when I'm ready to call it quits with her, she goes and does something almost cute.

"Fine. Work on the website if you want to." I wave at Kenzie as we get in my car.

She just waits by her mailbox while we back out onto the street, and right before we turn the corner, I sneak a peek in my rearview mirror to find her still standing there, like she can't move. I don't understand how we can be having a great time one moment, then like a switch, she flips into an ice-cold princess. Though I told her not to do my website, I really need it, even if it means losing her as a partner. As much as she drives me crazy, she's under my skin and there to stay. And I could kick myself for wanting her in my life when I know she'll hurt me.

Chapter 19

When my alarm blares Monday morning, I want to throw it across the room. Ever since our little blowup on Saturday, I've spent every single moment working on David's website. I don't care if he said he doesn't want me to. He's going to be so psyched when he sees it because it is awesome. And since I don't do anything halfway, I took the time to check out other websites for ideas and came up with something edgy, easy to navigate, and more importantly, easy for him to update without having to bug me every five minutes.

I yawn, drag myself out of bed, and stumble to the bathroom, bumping into Michael along the way.

"You look like death warmed over."

"I feel like it, but I got David's band website done."

"Can I see it?"

"Later. I need to wash up. I got in the zone, and to tell you the truth, I don't remember if I took a shower yesterday."

He sniffs my armpits. "Yeah... not likely."

"Ugh."

Right before I close the bathroom door, Michael adds, "You did the right thing by helping Shaw."

"It was purely for selfish reasons. In exchange, he'll finish our class project."

Michael frowns, but I don't care if he disapproves. That was the deal, and in less than one hour, I will be free of the likes of David Shaw. He'll get what he wants, and I'll get space. I'm sure he'll do fine on the project because he has as much to gain from getting a good grade as I do.

"So you're relinquishing control over something in your life?"

I roll my eyes. "It's the lesser of two evils."

"Whatever," he says, his voice fading as I shut the bathroom door.

Once I'm shower fresh, I throw my laptop in my book bag and rush down the stairs, where Michael waits for me.

"Ready?"

"Yep."

He's silent the entire way to school, which is odd. His white knuckles make me think he's angry about something, and that something is probably me.

"What's up, bro?"

Michael shrugs. "Just thinking you are usually such a by-the-rules kind of person. I can't believe you're going to let David do all the work while you sit back and get credit for it."

As if it's any of his business. "Listen. We've done a good portion of it together. Besides, this was his idea."

"I still think it sucks, and I'm not sure what you said to him, but the last band practice was not fun at all. He was all moody and grumpy."

"See? All the better that we don't have to interact anymore." I pat my book bag. "And I'll show him the website today. He'll love it so much, he'll thank me. It's truly a win-win situation."

"If you say so."

I stare out the window and think back to our last few conversations. At times, David and I are so in sync with one another that it really tests my color theory. Then, at the drop of a hat, we are at odds with one another. It's like we're fire and ice, and I'm sure he would think I am the ice in that analogy, but those situations are completely in alignment with my synesthesia.

Michael pulls into the school parking lot, and I don't even let him turn off the car before I'm out the door, hustling into the building. As soon as homeroom is over, I race-walk to my first-period class. David is already sitting at his usual desk, head down, writing in the project packet. Maybe we both got a lot done this weekend. I slide down the aisle past him, and he never glances my way. When I plop down in the seat behind him, Michael enters. While I fire up my laptop, David fist-bumps Michael, and they yammer on and on about some crazy song they're working on.

I clear my throat extra loud, and they both stop talking to turn my way.

"I have something to show you." I tap on the keyboard to get to his WordPress website. "Now, I know you said not to work on it, but I did anyway."

David huffs.

"I spent all weekend on this, so I hope you like it. Write this down. The domain name is NashTrash, and the password is NashTrash. You can change that whenever you want."

After a few more taps, I wait for the site to load. While the circle of impatience twirls, I give David a smirk. I hear a bing! and turn my laptop toward him.

"See what you think."

He scrunches his brow as Michael leans in close to view my beautiful website.

David cocks his head. "It's interesting, to say the least."

Tiffany and Harper walk into the room, and of course, they have to see what the guys are gawking about. Tiffany gasps, and Harper lets out a cackle.

Michael's jaw drops. "Sis, he's trying to get into college, not start a porn business."

"What?" I whip the laptop around to see a bunch of scantily clad women all over the website. "Oh my gosh." In a panic, I log out then back in. "There has to be a mistake."

When the NashTrash website pops back up, nothing I created is there. It's been replaced with boobs. They are all over the screen again—lots of them, big ones everywhere. "I don't understand."

Tiffany yells to the class, "Y'all got to see this!"

Everyone gathers round to see the hideous display of naked women taking up residence on my laptop.

Dylan whistles. "Is that you?"

Heat flames my face, and my ears burn. "God, no. Of course not."

Tiffany huffs. "If they were hers, they wouldn't even take up one-fourth of the screen."

If I didn't care so much about my laptop, I would hurl it toward her face.

Michael pops David on the shoulder. "Good luck with this." He climbs over a desk to get to Mollie while I sit there, jaw open, trying my best not to look at boobs.

"I..." I slam the laptop shut. "I don't know what happened."

With a straight face, he says, "You may think this website is a joke, but it's not to me."

"But I—"

"Never mind. I said I'll do it myself. I thought I could trust you, but it's completely obvious you want me to fail."

I jerk on his arm, but he pulls away.

"That's not true. I don't know what happened. Tonight, I'll figure it out, and I'll show you. I promise."

He throws up a hand. "Don't bother."

Tiffany tsks. "You wouldn't have this trouble if you were paired with me."

David breaks the wooden pencil he's holding.

Maybe it's the school's Wi-Fi connection. It has to be because everything I did, all the hard work I put into it, is gone. Not one trace remains of any of the pages I created. Tears prickle my eyes. "I'll figure it out tonight. I promise."

"I said don't bother." He goes back to working on the packet.

"So... about our project."

David throws his head back and lets out a wicked cackle. "You are unbelievable." He swings around to face me. "For your information, I spent a lot of time on the project this weekend, unlike you, who used your time trying to sabotage any chance of me getting a scholarship."

"That's not true."

"But because of your antics, you're still stuck with me."

He sticks his tongue out like a five-year-old, and I do the same.

"Fine. But I know what I did, and I'll prove it to you as soon as I get home."

Mr. Carter enters the room, carrying an egg carton. Miss Peters, the art teacher, pushes a cart loaded down with supplies. Construction paper hangs over the side while a box of glue sticks teeters on the edge, daring to escape the cart. She waves as she leaves.

Eli yells, "Breakfast?"

Mr. Carter snorts. "You wish. The next assignment is going to be about child raising." He opens the egg carton and passes it down the first aisle. "I took the liberty of draining the contents of the eggs myself because I'm no fool. The last thing I need is a couple to have an egg fight." He stares at Tiffany and Rhett.

Rhett groans. "Darn it. I think Tif's hair would look lovely with a slimy golden sheen."

Tiffany pins him down with a stare. "Don't even think about it."

Mr. Carter stares at the ceiling and groans as if he's already regretting this assignment. "The process is quite time-consuming, so I think you all should appreciate everything I did to keep you from being exposed to salmonella."

Mollie cringes. "Thanks."

"Today, you and your partner will decorate your baby, name it, and decide on the care plan for the next three days. Use the art supplies to decorate him or her really pretty and also design a system to carry your precious child. Here are the rules. You cannot leave the child unattended. Not even to go to the bathroom. In the event that nature calls, you must either take it with you or hand it off to the other parent. Keep track of who has the child at all times. And don't break the egg. If you and your partner can make it to Friday with your child unbroken and well cared for, you get bonus points on your project. If I find out you stuck your egg on the shelf and didn't move it for three days..."

The class groans. I guess we all had the same idea.

"You will lose a full letter grade, so I suggest you video your family out and about with your child. Make sure it's time and date stamped."

Tiffany raises her hand. "Mr. Carter, can I hire a nanny?"

"Absolutely not."

I glance over at Mollie. She claps and wiggles in her seat. The rest of us sit still as the assignment sinks into our brains.

Mr. Carter rubs his hands together. "Chop-chop. Get going."

David slowly turns to face me.

With a cringeworthy grin, I say, "It's a boy?"

He rolls his eyes. "Let's go meet our son."

Tiffany pushes Rhett out of the way. "Let me get the baby. You'll drop her the first day."

"Fine by me."

Tif pets the stupid egg like it's a real child. "There, there. Mommy's here."

David turns to me and mouths, "What the...?"

I bite my lip to keep from laughing at Tiffany. David peers over the carton and inspects the eggs. He touches each one until he taps the last one. He glances toward me. "What do you think?"

"It's fine by me."

His large hand gingerly picks up the egg and holds it out to me. "Our child is much better than *fine*."

"It's an egg. In fact, it's not even an egg. It's an eggshell."

"Hush, wife. Don't talk about my son that way."

I hold the egg while he pilfers the art supplies, bringing back various items to his desk.

"I think Walter is a good name."

Ew. "I don't think so."

"Noah, Chad, Brad, Fred." He stares at the ceiling.

"No."

"Then, what do you suggest? David Junior? DJ for short?"

Heavens no. Ugggggly.

I tap my finger to my lip, and his eyes drift to my mouth.

"How about Max?" The M is a very pretty dark purple.

He blinks then swallows. "Max Shaw doesn't sound good together." He smiles. "How about Aiden?" He holds his fist out for me to bump. I guess he doesn't hold a grudge for long.

"Perfect." I bump his fist as we go about decorating our little Aiden. After a moment of silence, I say, "I don't know what happened to your website. I promise I worked on it all weekend."

"Whatever. I'll figure something out." His words don't match his body language, which has turned into shoulders drawn in and a defeated look on his face.

"I said I'll fix it, and I will. I want you to go to Bellevue if that's where you want to go."

He chuckles under his breath. "Rhett thought those were your boobs."

Heat rises on my neck, turning my ears into fire lobes. "Well, like Tif said—"

"Your boobs are fine."

We lock eyes.

"What I meant was… never mind."

"Let's focus on our baby."

For the remainder of the class, he glues yellow yarn on the egg for hair, and I make a tiny basket made out of blue-and-green paper because they are a pretty combination. After I stuff the little basket with tissue paper, we place our egg inside then tape a few more strips of construction paper on top to keep him from escaping. I hold the egg basket out for Mr. Carter to see. He nods in approval.

"So, do you want me to take the first shift?"

I shake my head. "I will since I'm already in the dog house. Little Aiden will keep me company while I recreate NashTrash-dot-com."

"Okay, but let me know when you have to pee, and I'll come over to watch our little son."

"What about sleep?"

David's eyes twinkle. "Carter didn't give us specific instructions about that. What do you suggest?"

I squeeze my eyes shut, but all I see in my mind is David's face and those bouncy boobs. When I open my eyes, he's still staring at me. "I, uh... we'll have to, uh..."

"I'll tell you what. We'll take shifts. You watch him until either your eyes can't stay open, or your bladder is full. Then I'll take over. I don't mind if he watches me pee."

"Okay, this conversation is over. I'll take him home with me, and I'll text you when I'm ready to do the switcheroo. Good thing we live across the street from each other."

He nods. "Sounds like a plan."

The bell rings, and I throw my stuff in my bag. Dylan drops his egg before he can even get out the door. Harper whacks him on the arm. "You are impossible."

David chuckles.

I tap him on the shoulder and hold out our egg basket. "Watch Aiden while I go to the restroom."

"Yes, ma'am."

I think I've pulled myself out of the doghouse again. It shouldn't matter to me if he's mad or not, but for some reason, it does. As soon as I fix his website, it won't matter anymore anyway.

Chapter 20

One minute, Kenzie makes me so mad I could break our egg child with my stare. The next, I want to kiss her senseless. And I think she caught me staring at her lips. This project is making me miserable, but it is what it is. I don't think she created that awful boob-filled website on purpose. She was as shocked as I was, so I'm pretty sure it was not what she had designed. This little snafu only delays my application to Bellevue as well as the required time working with me on our project.

While she's on egg duty, I get to practice with the band. As I make my way through Hamilton and Kenzie's house, I notice our egg baby on the kitchen counter. Kenzie's head is buried in the refrigerator as she searches for something.

"Don't let our child get too close to that stove."

She jumps at the sound of my voice and bumps her head on a shelf. "Ow." Pulling out her ingredients, she places the egg a little farther from the stove. "How very parental of you to notice something like that."

"Well, I take care of Fi a lot, so it must come naturally."

She points to the garage door. "The rest of the motley crew is already assembled, eggs in hand, and before they ask you, I will not babysit all their eggs."

I salute her. "Yes, ma'am."

When I open the garage door, the guys are in a huddle. As soon as they see me, they jerk away, busying themselves with their instruments.

Hamilton smiles. "Hey, David. We were wondering, since Kenzie's taking care of your egg right now, would she—"

"Nope. My wife has already laid down the law."

Four heads sink low, and I let out a laugh, noticing four little baskets sitting on the floor next to the keyboard. "I guess you are all on daddy duty right now."

Rhett groans. "And mine is already cracked, but Mr. Carter said we still had to go through with the assignment. I'm passing it off to Tif in an hour. She said she would handle it overnight."

"Enough about eggs. Let's get this show on the road."

Dylan slides on his guitar strap. "That's an egg-cellent idea. Ha-ha."

"Sounds rotten to me." Rhett smiles, proud of his pun.

"Egg-scuse me. We are here to practice." Hamilton holds out his fist for someone to bump.

And I thought my dad had bad jokes. I shake my head. "Guys, stop it with the egg jokes. You're making my brain all scrambled."

"Boo," Hamilton says as Dylan throws a guitar pick at me.

For the next hour, we practice the latest song I wrote, and it doesn't sound like a screeching banshee. In fact, a pale-green splash of color fills my brain. While we work on the bridge, Kenzie rushes in, carrying our egg baby.

She shoves the basket into my hand and runs out. "Got to pee so bad, and I have a shy bladder."

"TMI, sis!" Hamilton yells at her retreating frame.

I stare down at our little Aiden egg. Kenzie added another layer of tissues to protect it better, and she put a little sock on it as a diaper. Cute. Hamilton clears his throat, breaking my thoughts.

"Are you going to rock it to sleep, or can we get back to rehearsal?"

I slide the egg basket onto my bass guitar neck and motion for Dylan to start with the bridge again. Little Aiden bobs to the song, but Michael gets a little too into his part because he bangs on the keyboard and knocks four little egg baskets onto the floor. A collective gasp runs through the garage.

"You killed Kurt." Dylan scoops his egg back into the basket.

Rhett shoves his to the side. "Yeah, yeah. Kids will disappoint you every chance they get."

I hold my egg basket as gingerly as possible as I rest my guitar on the stand. "I guess I'm a better dad than any of you guys."

I turn around and run smack-dab into Kenzie, the crumpled basket between us. When my startled expression meets hers, her mouth drops open.

"You killed Aiden."

I cringe and peel back the tissue paper, expecting to see tiny bits of Aiden in the bottom of the basket, but to my surprise, it's still intact, all except for a tiny crack on top. We both let out a sigh of relief. She snatches it from me. "I leave you for ten minutes, and this is what you do with our child?"

"Ha. Ten minutes? More like a full hour potty break."

She juts her chin up with a flat smile. "I got sidetracked." She motions with her head for me to follow her.

As soon as I enter the kitchen, the aroma of cheese and bacon overwhelms me. On the counter rests two dozen bone-shaped cookies.

"You *did* get side-tracked but in a good way."

When I go to pick one up, she smacks my hand. "Trust me, you won't like them as much as Catarina will. They have bacon and chicken broth in them."

I place it back and smile. "These look great."

She beams with pride. "It's a first attempt, but I think they turned out well. I took some photos for the final presentation."

"Good thinking."

We stare at each other, and the awkwardness is back.

Her gaze buzzes around the room. "I thought you might want to see if Catarina likes them. There's also a recipe for a peanut butter treat and an apple-carrot biscuit."

I make a face that causes her to laugh. "Let's stick to the bacon-and-chicken one for now." I pick up one of the treats that have cooled enough to not burn my hand and grab Kenzie with the other. "Let's go see firsthand if Cat likes them."

"Wait." She runs back to pick up the Aiden egg basket then hustles out right behind me. As we scoot across the street, she says, "David, I am so sorry about the website. I don't know what happened."

"Don't worry about it."

She stops me from walking up the steps to my house. "I promised you a website, and I will deliver. I really wasn't pranking you." She steps up onto the first step so we're eye to eye, and I force myself to keep my eyes trained on hers.

Don't look at her lips. Don't look at her lips.

She looks at mine. *Gah.*

I turn around and enter my house, whistling for Catarina. She barrels through the house, barking like she's a Doberman. When she sees me, she skids to a halt, slamming into my feet. As I lift her, her nose goes to town, already picking up a whiff of Kenzie's treat.

"Hello, girl. Kenzie has a special surprise for you."

While I document the moment with my phone, Kenzie holds the treat out to her as I put the critter back down. Cat's legs move even before her feet hit the ground. As soon as she makes traction, she races over to Kenzie's outstretched hand, snatches the goody, and races away. We follow her to her little bed in Fiona's room and watch as she scarfs it down, rooting around for any crumbs she might have left behind.

I prop my hand on the doorframe behind Kenzie. "I think she approves."

Kenzie nods. "That's a good thing because she's got enough for the next three weeks."

When I walk over to pet Catarina, she growls, making me jump back. "Okay. I think she likes them a little too much."

"Another member of the Shaw family who knows what she likes." Her eyebrows shoot up, but mine take a nosedive between my eyes. "I mean she knows what she likes to eat."

Still holding our egg, Kenzie takes one last look at Catarina. "I better bag those treats before one of the boys—"

"Oh no."

We run across the street, Kenzie holding tight to the egg basket. Surely the guys wouldn't eat dog treats. We burst into the house to find four teenage boys hovering over the kitchen counter, guzzling water. Kenzie side-eyes me.

"Kenz, I think you went a little heavy on the salt this time."

"Yep." Her word comes out as a squeak as she tosses the remaining cookies into a paper bag, never once locking eyes with me because if she did, we would both lose it.

She shoves the bag into my hand and points to the door. "I'll text you when it's your turn to watch Aiden."

I wink. "Goodnight, Mrs. Shaw."

"Aww," Dylan says, and he gets popped in the stomach by Kenzie's mean left hook.

MY HEAD HAS BARELY hit the pillow when my phone buzzes. I can't stop smiling when Kenzie's text says, *Honey, it's time to change your son's diaper.*

I text her back, *Be right there, pumpkin.*

When I'm almost to the door, Dad walks out of the kitchen, scaring the crap out of me.

"Where are you going?"

"Uh, I'm meeting Kenzie outside. It's my turn to watch the egg."

He shakes the cobwebs out of his head. "I don't think I want to know, but don't stay out late."

I roll my eyes. "Dad, it's only Kenzie, and I'll be back before you even get to your bedroom."

"True."

She waits under the streetlight, holding the basket, her mouth in a thin, flat line. "Hey." With two hands, she holds out the basket but doesn't let go even when I have a good grip on it.

"You okay?"

Kenzie shrugs and turns back to her house. "Collin is in there, and I can never sleep for thinking about what they must be doing."

I crinkle my nose, and she grins.

"You want to hang out with me for a little bit, until you're so tired your brain can't think anymore?"

Her eyes grow big. "Can I?"

"Sure. Come on." I take a step toward my house but realize she's not following me.

"I don't know."

"Your choice."

She folds her arms over her chest. "What about your dad?"

"We're not going to do anything he wouldn't approve of unless that's what you…"

Kenzie shakes her head fast. "Lord, no. I just know it's kind of late. Never mind. I'll put earbuds in my ears."

Before she can take off, I touch her arm. "Kenzie, come on. It's fine. We'll stay in the den and watch some television until you get sleepy. I've got some very salty dog treats in case you get hungry."

A giggle bubbles out of her mouth. "Okay."

As we tiptoe into the house, Dad stands at the door, waiting for me. "Hello, Mackenzie."

"Hey, Mr. Shaw."

I jerk a thumb over my shoulder toward Kenzie. "We're going to watch some TV if it's okay with you."

"Sure. In the den. With the door open. And don't stay up too late."

Well, that wasn't awkward at all.

She settles in on one end of the couch, and I sit on the other as I flip through shows on Netflix. We settle on the TV show *Riverdale*, and before we get ten minutes into the first episode, she dozes off with her feet in my lap. On instinct, I rub them, hoping I don't wake her. She looks so peaceful when she's zonked out like that, like she's not battling inner conflicts.

My mind races back to a time when she, Hamilton, and I used to have indoor campouts in this very room. Dad would move the furniture out, and we would pitch a tent. We had a tiny travel television that we would huddle around and eat s'mores my mom made in the microwave while it rained outside.

Kenzie lets out a sigh, and I wish I could snuggle in next to her. But I know my place. Catarina, on the other hand, doesn't know the unspoken rule, and she jumps up on the couch and snuggles in behind Kenzie's knees before she lets out a sigh of satisfaction. I scratch behind Catarina's ears, and out of the blue, Kenzie's hand covers mine to do the same thing. Her eyes flutter open and land on mine. For the faintest moment, all is right with the world. Until she slides her hand away and sits up, rubbing her eyes.

"I better go."

As I walk her across the street in silence, I wonder what's going on in her mind. We stand on her porch, neither of us saying anything or moving. I take a step closer to her, and she doesn't back away. I take another, and her breath hitches. My heart pounds like crazy, and her breaths are short and rapid. I want to kiss her so bad right now, I can't stand it.

Right as I lean down to place my lips on hers, she gasps. "Oh no."

I jerk away from her. "What's wrong?"

"We left Aiden all alone."

I throw my head back with laughter. "I won't tell if you won't."

She opens her door and whispers, "It's our little secret."

One step forward.

Chapter 21

In almost complete darkness, I lean back against the wooden door, doing my best to calm my breaths. David almost kissed me, and what's worse than the thought of his lips on mine is that I wanted them there. He's probably laughing his butt off right now at how I was gawking at his mouth, begging for him to close the space between us. I never noticed how perfect and plump his lips are. To keep things in order and uncomplicated, I need to finish his website soon.

"Where have you been?" Michael's words make me jump. He scratches his chin.

"You scared me." I sink into the couch and groan. "Why are you lurking in the dark?"

"Because I live here. I fell asleep on the couch."

Looking around the house, I ask, "Is he still here?"

"Collin? Yeah. So?" He flops down next to me and stretches his legs until his stinky feet are in my lap.

I swat them away. "He's disgusting, that's why."

Sticking his big toe in my ear, Michael says, "He's not that bad."

I squeeze his Achilles tendon, making him jerk his foot away from me.

"If you took the time to get to know him, you'd realize he's a pretty cool dude."

I roll my eyes. "Cool? Our mom does not need cool. She needs dependable, trustworthy, and stable."

Michael chuckles. "And you think the only person who can be all those things to Mom is Dad?"

"Exactly."

"Not going to happen."

"Yes, it is."

"You didn't answer my question. Where were you?"

Crap. I was hoping that with my misdirection, he would forget his original question. "I went out."

"You? Out?"

I nod. "Yeah. Out."

He flicks on the lamp next to him and pins me with his stare. His evil death gaze always squeezes the truth out of me. The trick is to not look him in the eye, so I focus on my clenched fists instead. He clears his throat, and on instinct, I glance up at him.

"Fine. I was at David's house."

His jaw practically hits the floor. "You were at David's house? Were you reminding him how much you hate him or something?"

"Shut up. No. I needed... a friend. We watched *Riverdale* until I fell asleep."

"Well, he does have that impact on girls."

I snort. "I bet he does. Anyway. As much as I hate to admit it, it felt good to hang with him again."

He leans forward and pinches my arm.

I jerk my arm back. "Ow. What was that for?"

"Just checking to see if I was dreaming."

"You're supposed to pinch yourself, not someone else."

He grins and goes in for another pinch, but I'm prepared this time. I ball up like a roly-poly so he can't find any vulnerable spots.

"You and David. Friends. Wow. I never thought I'd see that day."

"And if you ever repeat that, I'll tell Mollie you used to have the biggest crush on Lizzie McGuire. Besides, we're not *friends*. I can't let that happen. We are friendly. That's it. I have to get that website finished so I can unfriend him."

He blinks and stares at me. "Why would you want to do that?"

"You know why."

Michael groans and rests his head back on the couch. "Sis. Stop with the color crap. Just let life happen."

"Nope. I can't leave things to chance. It will be a disaster if I do."

"Kind of like that website?"

I throw my hands in the air. "Ugh. All that hard work down the drain."

He pats my leg. "I warned you that downloading all those porn videos was going to bite you on the butt one day."

"I do not download porn videos."

He lets out a yawn and stands. "Let me see your laptop. Five bucks says you have at least ten viruses."

I stand and march to my room. "You're on."

Not five minutes later, Michael struts around my room like a peacock. He holds his hand out right under my nose. "Pay up, doofus. Told ya."

I still gawk at the results of the virus scanner Michael ran. "Unbelievable. Can you recover the files?"

"If it was a file, like on your hard drive, maybe. But you were working on the web. It saved the latest version, so I can't help you there."

My hopes fade. "So, I really do have to start over?"

He pats me on the back. "Sorry, sis. Looks that way."

Like a six-year-old, I stick my tongue out at him. But I know he's right, so I shove him out of my room and settle in on my bed to recreate the website, but this time, I'll make sure I save every time I add new content.

After two hours of sitting cross-legged on my bed, hunched over the laptop, I'm in serious need of a break. I stand up to stretch when I notice a faint light on in David's bedroom across the street. Hoping he's not asleep, I take a chance and call his phone number.

He picks up on the first ring. "Still awake?"

"Yeah. But I put my insomnia to good use and made some serious progress on the NashTrash website, version 2.0."

"No nudie shots this time?"

I pull my curtains back to find him standing in front of his window. He waves.

"Don't remind me. That was awful. Anyway, I was thinking… if you want, you could come over and see what I've done so far. And bring Aiden."

He chuckles. "He does need some time with his mother."

"Don't come to the door. Do like we used to do."

I see him slide out his window and jog across the street. "The window?"

"Yeah. For old time's sake." *Why am I doing this to myself? David is an ugly word, remember?*

"Whatever, Mrs. Shaw."

He must think it's a booty call when all I want to do is show him the website without waking up the entire house. Maybe I should just meet him on the front porch. But before I slip on my flip-flops, the standard tap, tap-tap, tap-tap-tap echoes through my room, indicating he's already at my window.

Crap. Okay, Kenzie. You made your bed. Now lie in it.

The words *bed*, *lie*, and *David* should never be in the same sentence. I fling the window open, and he pops in like he used to all those years earlier. He sets the egg basket down on my dresser as he scans my room, taking in the posters of One Direction and Portugal. The Man bands. When he spots my REM poster, he laughs.

"You'll never get rid of that, will you?"

"They never go out of style. Get it? Harry Styles." I point to One Direction. "At least my Justin Bieber phase is over."

"It's about time." His eyes land on the laptop on my bed. "Show me the goods. I mean, show me the website." His face has streaks of red across it.

I sit on the edge of my bed, slide the laptop toward me, and drop it into his lap. "You are going to learn your way around this thing before another boob shot shows up."

He snorts. "That was so funny."

"Was not." I point to the log-in. "User name is NashTrash. Password is NashTrash. The *N* and the *T* are capitalized."

With his knees touching, he pecks away at the keyboard. He looks more like Schroeder from the *Peanuts* cartoon than my brother's best friend. When the website loads, his eyes grow big. "Wow."

I check over his shoulder to make sure he's wowing about my impressive web-design skills and not another nip-slip shot. He clicks through the menu in silence, and when he gets to the bios, he sees the Batman photo again. He smirks at me.

Holding up my hands in defense, I say, "I'm not done, all right?"

David gazes at me, making the room suddenly feel extremely small and without any available oxygen. "Kenz, I don't know what to say."

"Say you love it."

He nudges me with his shoulder then closes the laptop before he hands it off to me. "I do love it." He clears his throat. "I made some more progress on the assignment. You'll be happy to know we applied for a fake business loan, put a down payment on the shop, and registered a business name. How's that for progress?"

"Impressive." I let out an ugly yawn. "But I think I need my beauty sleep."

"Never, but I do." He winks.

Gah.

Before he slips out the bedroom window, he leans down and kisses me on the cheek. I don't even have a chance to react or smack him, and

I'm not sure I would have anyway. His warm lips on my skin weren't bad. At all.

"Thanks."

"Thank you for keeping me occupied and not thinking about Mom and her you-know-what." My eyebrows shoot up. "I didn't mean occupied like you were doing anything *to* me or *with* me. I meant, just... never mind. I'll stop talking now."

After a soft, sexy chuckle, he slips out the window and jogs across the street. With the sleekness of a cat, he takes one leap and climbs into his window. Part of me wants him to wave from his window, but another part of me is relieved he doesn't. It would have been nice and confusing all at the same time.

I need to finish the website, hand it off to David, and get back to my real life, where colors help guide my choices. It's crystal clear that leaving things up to me to do whatever feels right at the moment is not the wisest decision. Here I am hanging out with David, not hating him, and actually kind of liking him, of all things. I know he'll disappoint me. It's only a matter of time, so I need to reel in my stupid girly emotions, let my process do the work, and all will end well. But his lips felt so pretty.

Chapter 22

If Kenzie got as little sleep as I did, she's going to look like a hot mess. Fiona giggled when she saw the dark circles under my eyes, and Dad just shook his head, probably not wanting to ask in front of Fi how late Kenzie and I stayed up and what we were doing. I wish it was as interesting as they assumed.

I rotate my head in circles, trying to get the kink out of my neck. The tossing and turning I did after the almost kiss are going to cost me. My physics average is going to tank today if Mr. Pillers surprises us with a pop quiz. All night, I kept trying to figure out what was going through Kenzie's mind when we stood on her front porch, so close I could feel her breath. Maybe I'm kidding myself, but I would bet a dime to a donut that she wanted me to kiss her. That darn egg-child messed up our magic.

When I slide my head down onto my desk, I close my eyes and hope I don't start snoring. Harper's screechy voice doesn't even bother me. But the whiff of Kenzie's peach shampoo makes me completely alert. She plops our egg baby's basket onto my desk next to my head.

"You're on daddy duty now."

She sinks into her seat, and I get my first glimpse of her frazzled appearance. Yep. She tossed and turned the same as me.

"No problem. You look tired."

Kenzie waves me off. "It's tough being a mother."

I belt out a laugh. "I can only imagine. Little Aiden behaves so well for me. I don't know what your problem is."

She lets out a yawn. "Ha-ha."

While the rest of the bleary-eyed class filters into the room, Mr. Carter slides in and starts passing out a sheet of paper.

"Okay, today's assignment is resolving conflict. Take one, and pass it back." As soon as we all have one, he adds, "Here's our situation. You and your spouse have been married for three years now. You might have a child. Money is tight, and one of you has a spending problem. The other wants to hang out with friends rather than be at home helping with the child. Tensions rise. Work with your partner to figure out what the tipping point is. How would you react to your partner when you get angry? How could you react differently, and how would you prevent this from happening in the first place? Go."

I turn around and quirk an eyebrow. "So, Kenz, are you the spender or the party person?"

"Oh, I'm the party girl. That's for sure." She reads over the paper. "Well, I would probably get upset with you because you should know better than to hang out on Facebook Marketplace all day. We're on a fixed budget, you know."

My jaw drops. "So, hanging out with the girls isn't going to cost money?"

"Nope. I'll get guys to buy all my drinks."

"You better not."

Her eyes dance. "Why not? I'm not going to do anything with them. It's their problem if they pay for my drinks."

I shake my head. "My wife is not going to take drinks from random strangers. They prey on pretty young things like yourself."

She blinks, and her face becomes pale. "You think I'm pretty?"

"Of course. I'm not marrying a hag. So, no free drinks. Got it? If you go out with the girls, you pay for your drinks."

Kenzie doodles on the paper. "But that makes the financial situation worse."

"So, you go out with friends and charge a big bar bill. I am at home watching egg baby, buying Ginsu knives and the latest PlayStation console that we don't need—or you think we don't need. Is that our situation?"

"Yep. But it's probably the other way around. You spend, and I get mad and take it out on the family. I go to the bar, pick up the first guy I find, and before we know it, we're deciding which lamp is mine and if you keep the vase your mother gave us as an anniversary present. All the while, little Aiden is left hating both parents."

I scoot away from her. "Wow. You've thought this one through." More like she's lived this before. "All right. I see how this could happen, and we know where this could end up. So what if we back up a step, go back to the budget, and set aside some play money? You have money to go out with girls, a place where men won't hit on my woman."

She rolls her eyes.

"And I get a little bit of money to do what I want with. If we stray from our budget, the credit cards get buried in a drawer until the balance is paid off."

Her breaths become erratic. "I hate money."

"Most people love money. And it's kind of how our system works in this country. You make money. You use it to pay the bills. It's a necessary evil."

Kenzie snorts. "Oh, it's evil all right." She looks off toward Michael. He and Mollie have their heads stuck together, working on the project, laughing. "What's the one thing you'll do differently from your parents when you do get married?"

"Easy. Not die."

She covers my hand with hers. "That's technically impossible, you know that, right?"

"What would you do?"

"I would communicate. Maybe too much, which will be just as bad. My parents lived separate lives under the same roof because they never talked. If they would just come together and talk."

"Kenz, talking doesn't always solve the problems."

She snatches her hand away. "It wouldn't hurt."

"I agree. But some people shouldn't have gotten married in the first place."

Kenzie stands up so fast her chair tumbles over behind her, causing everyone in the room to stare at us.

"You take that back."

I hold my hands out in defense. "I wasn't talking about any couple in particular."

"Oh, yes you were."

"Kenz," Hamilton says in a warning tone.

"Oh, hush, Michael. You know he's talking about our parents."

Mr. Carter stands in front of Kenzie. "This is a what-if scenario. Don't go down the reality road, okay, Miss Hamilton?"

"Whatever." She turns her chair upright and slumps back into it, sneering my way. In a whisper, she says, "Just so you know, my parents are very compatible and will get back together real soon. You'll see."

"Okay." I'm not sure how we got here, but I'm willing to say anything to get her to calm down. I point to the paper. "Can we just finish the assignment?"

"Considering I am ninety-nine percent finished with your website, you can do ninety-nine percent of the assignment." She smirks as she crosses her arms over her chest.

"Fine." I scoot my chair back to face the front of the class and scribble on the page like a madman. She's going to wring my neck when she finds out my play money budget is twice as much as hers. If she's going to be a jerk, I can be a bigger one.

"Someone didn't take their Midol today."

I snap my head around to see Eli grinning like a buffoon. I stand to walk over to him, but Mr. Carter holds me back.

"Guys, this is supposed to be a fun assignment. Chill before I send everyone to detention."

"I am not going to detention because of that train wreck!" Tif yells from across the room. She has worked long and hard on the perfect head wag.

I sneak a peek at Hamilton. His jaw clenches. "Rhett, you better reel in your wife before I get arrested for punching a girl."

Thanks, Hamilton. "Ditto. Mr. Carter, do you mind if I use the restroom?"

He motions toward the door. "I think that would be a good idea."

I pick up my book bag and the egg basket and slam the door shut behind me as I storm down the hallway, past the bathroom, and out of the school. As I stomp toward my car, I realize I've never cut class before. This will look super awesome on my record, and if I get caught, I can probably kiss that scholarship goodbye, but right now, I don't care. I need to decompress, so I climb into the driver's seat, and instead of leaving campus, I recline the seat and focus on the roof of my car, trying to relax.

The project on conflict resolution sure did bring out the worst in me and Kenzie. She's got some deep-rooted feelings about her parents and truly believes they will reconcile. According to Hamilton, that will never happen. I fling a forearm over my eyes and try to drown out the noise in my brain. A knock on the window scares me so much I almost wish I had stopped at the bathroom instead of leaving.

Hamilton stands at the passenger door and yells, "Unlock the door!"

I lean over and unlock it so he can sit next to me. He follows suit and reclines the seat. "Ahh. Silence."

"Yeah. I was about to explode."

He chuckles. "I noticed. You want some advice?"

"Nope, but I know you're going to give it to me anyway, so knock yourself out."

He flings his arms over his head and closes his eyes. "Tif's only trying to get a rise out of you and Kenz, so don't let her win."

"I know."

"After that Midol comment, I'll deal with Eli. That was low. But you have to learn how to handle Kenzie and her warped fantasy about Mom and Dad getting back together. It's never going to happen, but no matter how much I try to convince her of it, she won't believe me. So I've pretty much given up. One day, it's going to hit her like a ton of bricks."

"It's just a stupid class assignment."

He wags his finger under my nose. "Not to her. It's causing her to think about what is wrong with our parents' relationship and reinforcing her way of thinking and that she thinks they'll get back together. I know my sister. She's filing all this away in the how-to-avoid-making-the-same-mistakes file."

I groan. "You know, I thought being paired with her was going to be the perfect way to break the ice. And there have been times when she's thawed and shown me who she used to be. But then she'll go right back into that freezer and shut me out." I shake my head in disgust. "It would have been easier getting paired with Tif."

"Bite your tongue. If Rhett ever heard you say that, he'd pay you money to switch places. I think he's on a hefty dose of antacids right now."

His words make me chuckle. "I guess. But Kenzie is never going to let me in completely. Even as recently as last night, I thought we were making progress." I close my eyes for fear of seeing his reaction. "I came very close to kissing her."

"Dude. And you lived to tell about it?"

"Yeah. But today, she's back to being closed off. I don't understand. Whenever we talk about the project, she gets all rigid in her thinking."

"You wouldn't understand, so don't even try." He glances down at his watch. "Bro, we need to get back inside before the bell rings."

"How did you get out of class?"

"Sometimes, my farts have perfect timing. I left a gas bomb, so everyone pretty much begged me to leave."

I scrunch my face. "Dude, you're nasty, but I am impressed."

He opens the door, and we walk toward the school. Thank goodness he didn't let one rip in my car. "What can I say? I have many hidden talents."

"Does your wife know about them?"

Hamilton laughs. "She does now."

I double over laughing. "I can imagine poor Mollie's face all scrunched up. But she's so into you. She won't care as long as you spend time with her."

He walks backward with a confused expression. "As my wife or as my sister's friend?"

"As your girlfriend. Just ask her out. You're perfect for each other."

His face flushes. "You think so?"

"You're an idiot."

Before we go our separate ways toward our second-period classes, he pops me on the back. "You're perfect for someone too. She just doesn't know it yet."

I snort as I head toward my calculus class. If he's talking about Kenzie, he's got it completely wrong. Some days, I think so. Other days, I think it's not worth my time. This project cannot be over soon enough. It's driving us both a little nutty.

Before I force myself to go to second period, I stop off at my locker. While I'm hunting around for last week's homework, Anne O'Reilly leans against the locker next to mine, her skirt showing off her long legs.

"Hey, David."

Anne and I have a bunch of classes together, but she's usually surrounded by her massive flock of friends. She knows who I am, but we run in different circles. The main reason I know her is by her voice over the intercom, giving the morning announcements every day. She's one of those girls who aren't into cheerleading or sports, but everyone knows her. She's nice and is always cheerful, which is way more than I would ever say about Kenzie.

"Hey."

"Can I ask you something?"

I look around to see if I'm being pranked. "Knock yourself out."

Anne pushes off the locker, and we walk side by side toward second period. "So, I heard about that crazy fake marriage project."

I groan. "Aren't you sad you don't have Mr. Carter?"

She giggles. "Nope. Not at all. But I know you're paired with Kenzie, and I was wondering, are you two dating?"

My calculus book slides out of my hand, and papers fly all over the hallway. Thank goodness I didn't drop the egg basket. "What? No. Why would you think that?"

Anne leans down to help me retrieve the mess I made. "I've always had the impression you had a thing for her, and now that you're paired, I was just wondering..."

"We are not dating." As sad as the words make me, it's the truth.

She flicks her eyes up at me and smiles. "Good. Do you want to do something tonight?"

This girl goes from zero to sixty in ten seconds flat. "I have band practice."

"We could go get something to eat after. What do you say?"

Mollie and Kenzie pass us in the hallway, and as soon as Kenzie sees me, her smile fades.

When they turn the corner, I look back at Anne. "Sure."

Anne bounces and pulls out a Sharpie. She yanks my arm toward her and writes her phone number on the inside of my forearm. "Call me as soon as you're done with your rehearsal, and I'll meet you at Pizza Perfect."

If this project has taught me anything, it's that Kenzie and I will never be more than frenemies. That's it. It's time to move on.

Chapter 23

The only bad part about having Mollie over while the guys practice is that I can't wear my noise-canceling headphones. So I have to endure the racket while my best friend rambles on about how much fun she and Michael are having. It's kind of cute seeing them all googly-eyed at each other finally.

Mollie steals a chocolate chip cookie while I add another batch to the oven.

"How's your project going?" she asks.

I shrug. "It's going. David's doing a lot of the project as per our agreement, but at times, we're forced to be in the same room together. It's kind of awkward, but I'm trying to be mature about it."

She stares a hole through me. "Mature? As in not liking a guy for no good reason?"

I nod.

"Real mature, Kenz. He can't be that bad."

Oh yes, he can. "You wouldn't understand."

She jerks a thumb over her shoulder toward the garage. "Anyone who has a voice like that cannot be all terrible."

My attention snaps to David's smooth-as-silk baritone floating through the air, singing one of his original songs—something about second chances, first dances. "He's okay."

"Okay? He's awesome, and he writes his own stuff."

I point a spatula at her. "Not all the time. I hear him run through a few Mumford and Sons songs every now and then."

Mollie snaps her fingers under my nose. "Ha. So you do listen."

I stuff a cookie in my mouth, and my eyes roll back in my head. "Kind of hard not to. It's right there."

She leans over the counter and whispers, "Rumor has it, Anne O'Reilly has her sights set on David."

My face gets all scrunched up like I ate a bunch of lemons. Anne's name is all ugly, thus I've avoided her. The brown A next to bright pink is hideous. Most people seem to like her, but I just can't get past her name.

"Surely he has better things to do with his time."

"Like hang out with someone who doesn't like him?" She quirks an eyebrow.

"Not my fault. It's this stupid project." I point to the kitchen table, where our egg babies rest. "And that. I cannot wait for *that* part to be over."

Mollie lets out a starstruck sigh. "Michael is such a good daddy."

"It's an egg. It's not even an egg. It's an eggshell with some yarn for hair."

She sits up taller and juts her chin high. "I know, but it shows what he would be like if it were a real child. His attention to detail, his ability to put someone's needs above his own. It's so romantic."

Her eye fluttering sends a wave of nausea over me.

I cover my mouth with my hand and pretend I'm about to throw up. "Please, don't say that stuff about my brother. I know you like him, and thank goodness he's finally getting past his shyness to show you his feelings, too, but there are a few things I don't want to know about him. So don't tell me how he makes your leg pop when he kisses or anything like that."

"It does."

While I slide the cookies onto a plate, I ask, "What does?"

"My leg. It pops when he kisses me."

I cover her mouth with my hand as she giggles. "You rat. Stop. It's gross."

"What's gross?"

We swing around to see the four guys standing there. They've already eyed my plate of cookies, so there's a good chance I can slide past this conversation with a little bit of chocolate temptation.

"Uh, the first batch of cookies." *Liar.*

Mollie cracks up and hands the plate over to Michael. Rhett and Dylan dive into the cookies, but David stands back.

"Are these human cookies?" David asks.

"Yes, they are."

Michael sneers, making him lose part of his cookie. "Oh, yeah, thanks a lot for not telling us about the dog treats. That was harsh."

I hold my hands out in front of me. "You didn't give me a chance."

"She's right," David adds. "Dudes, you know we have a dog bakery, so it's your own fault." He holds his fist out for me to bump. It's the least I can do.

Dylan clears his throat. "Like Kurt Cobain says—"

Rhett throws up his hands. "I'm out of here. He can't go one day without quoting Kurt Cobain."

Dylan shrugs. "It's true."

Rhett punches Dylan's arm. "I've got to go meet with my wife." He freezes then does a whole-body shiver. "Please don't ever let me say that again."

Michael plays an air violin as Rhett leaves. "Poor guy."

Dylan snorts. "Poor nothing. Harps is driving me over the edge."

Michael points at David. "Looks like we got good wives. Nothing to complain about."

David freezes me with his stare. "It could be worse. I better go. I have a date."

Now my jaw is on the floor. "What about Aiden?"

His eyebrows rise. "Can you watch him tonight, honey? It might be a little awkward bringing a child on a date. Don't you think?"

Bile rises in my throat. If he's going out with Anne, I think I'm going to hurl. "Fine. I'll watch him again tonight. But he's all yours tomorrow."

He winks as he heads for the door.

"Wait!" I yell right before he has a chance to leave. "I have something for Catarina." I pull out a zipped bag full of dog treats. "I made another batch. These have bananas in them. Let me know how she likes them."

His fingers brush mine as he takes the bag out of my hand. "Thanks. I'm sure she will devour them in one sitting if I let her."

He stares at me, and I can't think of a way to respond.

With a thin-lipped smile, I finally say, "Have fun on your *date*," then turn back to the kitchen to clean up my mess.

Mollie and Dylan make excuses to leave, and all that's left in the kitchen with me is Michael. I slam dishes around as I wash them. All the while, Michael sits on a barstool, watching me implode.

"I know you want to say something, so spit it out."

"No, I don't."

"Yes, you do."

The door opens, and we both whip our heads around to see Mom enter. She struggles as she carries four bags of groceries. "Hey there, my lovelies." She gives us both a kiss. "Don't make plans for dinner because Collin is coming over, and we're going to have a real meal together."

"Cool," Michael says.

"I'm super busy with school stuff." I hate lying to my mother, but I don't think I can handle being in the same room with Collin. The C is an okay shade of blue, but the white O and the light-gray Ls are ugly.

Michael sneers at me. "No, you aren't." He smiles at Mom. "We'll be here. Do you need any help?"

Mom bounces. She actually bounces like a teenager, like she hasn't done in years. "I thought you'd never ask. Mike, you start the pasta, and, Kenz, can you start cutting up the vegetables for the salad?"

"Whatever."

Maybe if I focus on chopping up cucumbers, I won't feel like chopping off any protruding parts on this home-wrecker.

MICHAEL AND COLLIN yammer on and on about computer processors and random-access memory while I push food around my plate, pretending to eat at least a few bites. Mom beams at Collin like he's the most awesome person in the whole wide world. Ugh.

Collin leans back in his chair and rests his arm behind Mom's shoulders, causing my blood to boil. Mom leans into him, and the few bites I did eat are about to make a repeat performance. Trying to think of a way to split up this cavity-inducing bubble they're in, I pretend to reach for a dinner roll. In the process, I accidentally-on-purpose knock over his wine glass, sending his drink into his lap. Everyone at the table jumps up. Mom grabs a dishtowel and starts patting his crotch. Not what I was going for.

"Oh dear, Cols, I'm so sorry. Why don't you go upstairs and change, and I'll soak your pants in stain remover?"

Michael stands. "Come on, Collin. I'm sure I've got an old pair of Dad's sweats you can wear."

"No!"

The three of them freeze to stare at me. He can't wear my dad's clothes. First, he's sleeping in my dad's bed, and now, he's wearing his clothes. It's too much.

Mom stomps over to me, and with her back to Collin, she says, "He can wear anything he wants. This is my house. In fact, it's either the old sweats, or he can walk around in his underwear."

I gasp.

Mom smirks like a trained teenager. "Your pick."

Collin clears his throat. "I think I should leave. That's probably best for right now."

You got that right.

Mom shakes her head and holds out a hand to stop him from leaving. "Nope. We are all going to play Monopoly."

My eyes get wide. Dad loves that game. "That game could go on for—"

"Hours." Mom grins over at Collin. "How about it, sweetie?"

Shoot me now.

Collin turns to Michael with a tentative expression. "What do you say?"

Hoping my twin telepathy kicks in, I stare at him. His twitchy grin tells me all I need to know.

"I would love to play."

"But it's a school night." *Good one, Kenzie.*

Collin takes in this dysfunctional family, and if I were him, I would cut and run at the first chance. He walks over to my mother and takes her face in his hands. And right in front of me, he kisses her. My head is about to explode. *How dare he do that?* Michael lets out a wolf whistle. When I get him alone, I'm going to punch him.

Collin nods. "She's right about school. Why don't we watch a movie? Kenzie can pick."

Now all eyes are on me. I don't want to eat with this man, and I don't want to play board games. And I certainly don't want to sit around watching a movie while my mother makes out with her boyfriend that is at least ten years younger than her. That's just gross, but I don't see a way out of this, so since he's given me permission to choose, the ball is in my court. And I know just the movie to get him running. He'll hate it. Most guys do. I know Michael despises it.

I stand straight and say, "Okay. Let's watch *The Princess Bride.*"

Michael and Mom groan, but Collin gets the biggest grin on his face.

He rushes around the room, pretending to sword fight. "I love that movie. Kenzie, as you wish!"

That didn't work out like I planned.

Chapter 24

It's been a long time since I've been on a date. I guess the last one I went on was with Tiffany, and that was a disaster. After band rehearsal, I rush home and jump in the shower, then shave my sparse scruff of facial hair.

Fiona walks past my room and does a double take. "Wow. Look at you." She sniffs the room. "And you smell good too. What's up with that?"

I pick her up and plop her down on my bed. "I have a date."

"Really. Where are you and Kenzie going? Can I go too?"

She tries to get up, but I shove her back down as I go in search of shoes that are of the non-sneaker type.

"It's not Kenzie. It's Anne. And no, you cannot go."

Fiona props herself up by her elbows. "Who is Anne?"

"A girl who kind of asked me out, if you must know."

She digs under the bed and tosses the left loafer my way. "Is Kenzie okay with it?"

I chuckle. "Kenzie isn't my real wife, and she certainly isn't my girlfriend. We are barely friends."

Fiona pouts. "I just thought..."

"You thought wrong."

She crosses her arms in a huff, and I sink down beside her. "I know you like Kenzie. And she likes you too. She just doesn't know it yet."

Catarina bounces into the room and takes a flying leap right into Fiona's outstretched arms.

"Cat likes Kenzie too."

"Stop with the matchmaking, Yente."

She scrunches her brow. "What's a Yente?"

"If you watched something other than *Prince Not-So-Charming*, you might know, but I don't have time to give you the synopsis of *Fiddler on the Roof*. Gotta run."

Still sitting in my room, she yells at me as I walk down the hallway, "You're making a big mistake!"

Just to tick her off, I sing the lyrics to her favorite show, "Keep calm, and put your crown on."

When I get to my car, I look down at my arm and realize I washed off Anne's phone number. That's just great. A girl is finally interested in me, and I muck it up. Hoping she will show up at Pizza Perfect anyway, I drive there. If nothing else, I'll order a pizza to take to Dad and Fi.

When I walk in, the first person I see is Anne.

She's behind the counter, waiting on customers. She grins as soon as our eyes meet. "You didn't call. I figured you changed your mind."

I roll up my sleeve to show her a clean arm. "I took a shower and lost your number."

She giggles. "A likely story."

"Hey, it's true." I scan the room. "I didn't know you work here."

She scoots around to my side of the counter and waves to the man in the back. "My dad owns this place. I'm here more than I'm at home." Anne tosses me a menu and motions for me to follow her to a booth. We both train our eyes on the menu until she flicks hers up over the laminated page. "How's the project going?"

"It's a lot more work than I expected."

"I bet. Harper complains about it. All. The. Time."

I sit back in the booth and rest the menu on the table. "I didn't know you and she were friends."

She shrugs.

A waiter stops by, and we order our pizza and drinks.

"We're friendly, but I wouldn't consider us friends. People think I have a lot of friends, but I don't. I just try to be nice to everyone."

"That's a good policy."

She takes off her work hat and rests it on the table. "Sorry I'm so sweaty. Dad needed me to help a little before the rush got here. It's Tune Tuesday."

"I've heard of Taco Tuesday but not Tune Tuesday."

Anne giggles. "Tune Tuesday is when my dad lets local bands take over the stage and do a small set. It brings in business on a normally slow night."

My eyes shoot up at the word "band." "Your dad lets—"

"Yeah. Most of them are pretty lousy, but now and then, we'll get something pretty good. Ever heard of The Frisbees?"

I fall back into my seat. "No way. They're huge and sell out concerts all the time."

"Yep. When they were first starting out, they played places like this all the time."

The Frisbees are on fire. I knew they were a local college band, but I guess I assumed they always played places bigger than this. The stage is barely big enough for two people.

"How did I not know this?"

The waiter returns with our drinks, and Anne shoots the paper off her straw at me, hitting me square in the face. "Because most people don't get out on Tuesdays. Or if they do, it's for tacos."

We fist-bump.

"Good one."

For the next few minutes, the conversation comes easy. Most of the time, she's in the driver's seat and doing the talking, but I don't mind. If she didn't ask a ton of questions, we would sit there staring at each other. That wouldn't be a problem either because she's pretty, even if she's sweaty.

"So, what do your parents do? You know my dad owns this lovely establishment, and my mother is a nurse at Centennial Hospital."

"Dad is an animal control officer."

"That must be hard. Does your mom work?"

"No."

Stuffing more pizza into my mouth to avoid the mom convo, I hope she changes the subject.

"You don't live with your mom, do you?"

I shake my head.

"Do you ever get to see her?"

"Never." My pulse quickens. I don't want to talk about Mom, and it is clear she has no idea about my situation.

She places a hand over mine and squeezes it. "That's awful. Where does she live?"

I jerk my hand away from her and guzzle down my iced tea. "In Woodmont Gardens Cemetery—or heaven if you believe in that stuff."

Her mouth flies open. "I didn't know."

I wave her off. "It's okay. It happened a long time ago. I guess I assumed everyone knew, but you must have moved here after middle school."

Anne fidgets with her napkin. "Tenth grade. I'm really sorry."

"Let's talk about something else."

"What happened to her?"

The waiter walks by, and I hand him my plate. I couldn't eat more if I tried. "I don't want to talk about it."

"Was it an accident?"

"Anne, let's talk about something else." Boy, she's pushier than I expected.

She nods. "You're right. I feel like a complete heel. I don't know what I would do without my mother. She's everything to me."

I let out a chuckle. "What happened to talking about something else?"

She slaps her forehead with her hand. "I am such a doofus. Sorry." She clears her throat, and a guy with a guitar walks in. Anne snaps her head around so fast I think she's going to give herself whiplash. "What kind of music does your band play?"

Finally, a topic I love talking about. "A little of everything. If Dylan had anything to do with it, we'd play nothing but Nirvana."

Anne laughs. "Nirvana is cool."

"We mostly play alt-rock. Some cover tunes. Some originals."

Her eyes shoot up. "That sounds great. I can ask my dad if he has a Tuesday slot open for a band."

Now she has my attention. "That would be awesome. You name the date, and we'll be there."

She holds out her hand, and we high five. "It's the least I can do since I was such a Debbie Downer before."

"Don't worry about it."

My phone buzzes, and I pull it out of my pocket to see the text. Kenzie's message says, *Aiden misses his daddy.*

"Your face lit up. Must be from someone special."

I didn't realize I was smiling. "Not really, but I probably should go. I've got stuff to do on my project."

She bounces out of the booth. "Yeah, I need to help Dad anyway. I'll let you know what he says about the band, but I'm sure he'll be okay with it. He'd rather have a crappy band than no band—not that yours is crappy."

I dust off the pizza crumbs as I stand. "You haven't heard us yet."

Anne walks me to my car, and we stand there in silence. I'm a bit out of practice, so I'm not sure what to do. I'm not even sure if this was a date or just two friends eating together.

She points to the restaurant. "I need to go. See you at school."

Thinking maybe it would be okay to kiss her on the cheek, I lean in. She scoots away and waves as she runs back into the restaurant. I'm not an expert on dates, but that was one of the oddest ever. I did get a gig out of it, or at least, I hope I did.

Chapter 25

In total darkness, I sit on my porch, waiting for David's car to roll down the street. He's on a date with Anne. If she wasn't so nice, I'd hate her. Everyone else likes her, unlike me. Most people give me a wide berth, and it normally works for me. It keeps the weirdos away. Mollie sees right through my attitude and so does Michael.

If he doesn't show up soon, I'm going to embarrass myself with a huge wet spot on the porch. I take some deep breaths and do my best to think of anything non-aquatic, but it's not helping. The lawn sprinklers across the street pop up and start spraying water mostly on the road. Freddie Jones' dog rambles by, stopping in my front yard to pee while my eyeballs feel like they are about to float out of their sockets.

A car door slams, almost scaring the pee out of me. David turns toward my house and motions with his finger for me to come over to him. "I know you're there, so you might as well stop trying to hide."

He is so annoying, but like a kid caught with their hand in a cookie jar, I look around as if he's talking to someone else. He laughs and walks toward the street.

"I was just checking out the stars. They are so pretty."

He stares up at the sky. "It's cloudy. Looks like it could rain any minute."

Jerk.

He climbs the steps to sit beside me, and we fall into a comfortable silence. I jump up. "Don't leave. I'll be right back."

I rush to the bathroom, do my business, then race into the kitchen to pick up a plastic container. Fearing he's gone back home, I dart outside and almost collide with him, still sitting in the same place. I hold out the container.

"Here, I made you some cinnamon rolls."

He peels open the container and takes a whiff of the contents. "Can I have one right now?"

"Just make sure there's at least one each for your dad and Fiona."

He takes one in his hand and rolls it out, dangling it in front of my face. "You want some?"

I can't say no to cinnamon, so I open my mouth, and he lowers the strip into my mouth. I bite off a hunk, then he eats a piece.

Through his moans of satisfaction, he says, "You are so good at this. If I was around you all the time, I'd be fat as the Pillsbury Dough Boy."

"Well, hanging out with Anne will keep that from happening." Crap. I didn't want to bring up her name.

He scrunches his eyes together and, with his thumb, removes something off my mouth. I'm probably covered in sticky icing. "Looks like you got something on your face. It's green." His eyes twinkle. "Mrs. Shaw, are you jealous?"

I shove his chest. "In your dreams. I don't care who you have a date with."

"Sure, you don't." He lets out a deep breath. "To tell you the truth, I'm so out of practice, I don't know how to act on a date. But honestly, it was very weird. The whole time I was with her tonight, it felt forced." He swallows a piece of cinnamon roll then adds, "I don't know why I told you that."

"Because we're friends."

He turns to me and even though it's just the light of the front porch, I see seriousness etched across his face. "Are we? If so, you have a very strange way of showing it."

I stare down at the container I'm still holding with the force of the Hulk. "Other than my brother, I only have one real friend. Mollie is the only one that takes me as I am, quirks and all. I've pushed everyone else away, and I can't explain my reasoning."

David slides a strand of hair behind my ear. "You push yourself away. We're still here. I'm still here."

I'm so glad I peed because his words coupled with his touch would have relaxed me enough to leave me sitting in a puddle right now. "Are you two dating now?" I gasp. "None of my business. Sorry."

He snatches another cinnamon roll and does the same thing with unrolling it and feeding me like a baby bird. "She's very nice. There is absolutely nothing wrong with her, but..." He shrugs. "We'll see."

"Your website is mostly done. Do you want to see it?"

With a huge grin on his face, he replies, "Heck yeah."

I toss the container into his lap and jump up. "I'll be right back."

When I return with my laptop, he's finishing off another cinnamon roll. He then licks the icing off his fingers. "Okay, Mr. Shaw, I hope you like this. No boob shots this time."

I drop down next to him, and he snaps his fingers. "Darn. A guy can dream, I guess."

While I power up my laptop, he gets a text message. He punches his fist in the air. I guess he got a second date.

"Okay, here is the link to your website."

I turn the laptop to him and grin at what I created. He scrunches up his brow. "It says, site not found."

Whipping the laptop around, I type the URL again. "I'm tired. I must have typed it in wrong." My jaw drops when it says the same thing again. "What is wrong with this laptop?"

I slam it shut and rock back and forth, holding my stomach. If I spent all that time working on his site again and it's not work-ing—*again*—I think I'll throw up.

He takes the laptop from me and places it on the porch. "Show me tomorrow when you aren't so tired. He grins big. "And you'll have something to add to the 'events' page."

"Really?"

"Yep. Annie's dad owns the Pizza Perfect restaurant. He lets local bands take over the stage on Tuesdays. She just texted me with the date."

One eyebrow shoots up. "Annie? So it's Annie now. Not Anne?"

"Out of all I just said, that's what you heard?" He flicks my nose. "You need some sleep, Mrs. Shaw."

He starts to stand, but I yank his arm, causing him to sit back down, this time even closer to me. "I'll add it to the website. I'm happy for you. It will be good exposure for you and will look much better on the website instead of a lame 'coming soon' placeholder."

"And you'll be done with having to deal with me. I'll finish the project, and we can go back to being nothing more than neighbors."

My heart sinks. I've started to really like our time together, and that surprises no one more than me. The fact that I won't have an excuse to talk to him or spend time with him kind of makes me melancholy. As much as I hate to admit it, David isn't so ugly after all.

But ugly people let me down.

"Yes. By tomorrow, we can shake hands and go our separate ways." I hold out my hand, and he takes it. He rubs the back of my hand, and a warm, tingly sensation runs up my spine. My eyes flick up to his, and we stare at one another. "But tonight..." His eyes get big with anticipation. "You are on daddy duty."

I remove my hand from his and pick up the egg basket behind me. His shoulders slump when I hand it to him.

With a low rumble of laughter, he says, "Yes, ma'am."

"Take care of our child."

He stands, and with the egg basket in one hand and the container of what's left of the cinnamon rolls in the other, he climbs down the steps. "I will always take care of our child. See you tomorrow, Kenz."

Unable to move off the porch, I watch his long, lanky legs carry him across the street and toward his house. Without turning around, he enters his home and shuts the door behind him. Like a statue, I remain in the same place, waiting until he turns on the lamp in his bedroom. I rush to my room and gawk out my window toward his. Through a partially closed sheer curtain, I see him take his shirt off and fling it across the room. He unbuckles his pants and slides out of them, leaving nothing but a pair of boxer briefs and a whole lot of muscular skin.

As if he feels someone watching, he closes the curtains completely, then turns off the light. I need to get my head examined because he's sweet, he's very easy on the eyes, and he likes me regardless of my weirdness.

Maybe I can warm up to him and forget my stupid rules about letters and colors. I will have to be colorblind. And he'll never have to know why I was so distant for so many years. The trick is to re-train my brain to make my own decisions and not let a system do it for me. I don't know if I'm brave enough to do it, but I have to try.

I storm into my brother's room and, in the darkness, sink onto his mattress. He jerks awake, and when he turns on his lamp and sees me, he flops back onto his pillow, breathing hard. "Jeez Louise. Are you trying to give me a heart attack?"

"Michael, what is wrong with me?"

"Well first off, you wake your brother up out of a deep sleep—"

"I'm not talking about that. But I am sorry. Why can't I like him?"

"Who?"

"David. That's who. He's nice, we get along when I don't get all grouchy, and for the first time in my life, I think I see what other girls see in him. He's pretty much a babe."

Michael covers his face with a pillow and groans. "Can we talk about this tomorrow?"

I snatch the pillow out of his grip. "I'm serious. Do I need therapy or something? Why haven't I seen this all along?"

He chuckles and covers his eyes with his forearm. "Sis, you do not need therapy. Your stupid color system is for the birds. You need to ditch it, and you'll be fine. You're just a little jealous that he spent time with Anne tonight."

"Ugh. He calls her *Annie*." I let out a sigh. "But she's nice and I'm not. They are perfect for each other."

Michael turns off the lamp then slides the sheet over his face. "Please go to sleep. Or at least, let me go to sleep."

I sit in the dark, and his breaths slow down. Right when I think he's asleep, I add, "I finished the website."

"Please go away."

"At least I think I did. My laptop doesn't recognize the URL."

"Sis, if you have another virus, I am going to ground you."

I pick at a fingernail. "Will you look at it?"

"Yes. I will look at it in the morning. Go to sleep."

"Thanks."

While I lie wide awake in my bed, I wonder if David is doing the same thing, or if he's wide awake, thinking of Anne. I deserve to be a lonely old cat lady because after years of blocking him from my life, he's figured out I'm not worth the trouble. Maybe Mollie will have some answers for me. Tomorrow, I'm going to figure out what's wrong with the website and decide how I really feel about David. I don't know where I stand with him, but the thought of him spending time with any other girl does bring out the green in me.

Chapter 26

If I look anything like I feel, I'm sure I look like an extra on The Walking Dead. I tossed and turned most of the night, and every time I got a glimpse of the egg baby, my mind drifted back to Kenzie. She is an enigma soft shell taco. She acts like she doesn't care about me, but then says we're friends. She doesn't want anything to do with me but gets all jealous when another girl looks my way.

Hamilton and Kenzie walk in fussing about something, and quite frankly, I'm too tired to care. Hamilton slips into the desk next to me as Kenzie walks past me to her usual first period desk. He tosses me a flash drive.

"Keep that in case your partner in crime messes up your website again. I've copied the code onto the flash drive as a backup because Miss I-Can't-Believe-I-Messed-It-up-Again messed it up again."

I swing around to see Kenzie slumped in her desk, arms crossed over her chest. "Remember, the URL wouldn't load last night? Well, Michael finally figured it out. I don't understand it, but it's working now."

The flash drive in my hand could hold my future. It also lets Kenzie free of our deal. "Thanks. Both of you."

"How did Aiden sleep last night?"

"Not at all. He kept me up, crying for his mother."

Kenzie rolls her eyes. "He's all yours now. I hope you get used to middle-of-the-night diaper changes."

I shake my head. "You are abandoning your child? You should be ashamed of yourself."

"But I'm not." She looks over to her brother. "Did he tell you the good news?"

"That we all get to sleep in during first period?" Hamilton lets out a huge yawn.

"No, silly. That *Annie* got you all a gig at Pizza Perfect."

Boy, I don't think she could put more venom into the way she said Anne's name.

Hamilton stares at me with a twinkle in his eye. "We got a paid gig?"

"Well, it's whatever is collected in tip money, but yeah. Next Tuesday."

He fist-bumps me. "Cool."

The rest of the class scoots in right as Mr. Carter shuts the door.

"Okay, everyone, please give me an update on your egg children." When no one answers, he stares at Harper.

She sneers over at Dylan. "He killed our baby."

Dylan wipes fake tears off his face. "Boo-hoo-hoo."

Tiffany huffs. "We didn't do any better."

"Us either," Mollie says. She looks over to Hamilton and mouths, "Sorry."

Mr. Carter scans the room. "Is there at least one couple with an intact egg child?"

I turn to look at Kenzie. Together we raise our hands.

"You two get ten points extra credit."

I punch my fists in the air. "Yes!"

Tiffany huffs.

Kenzie sticks her tongue out at her. "You're just jealous that my husband and I are masters at taking care of children. And there's that whole extra-credit bit, so yeah."

Adorable.

"Okay, class. You all can dispose of your egg babies."

Mollie pouts. Of course, she's become attached to her egg child even though it's been crushed for days.

"For the rest of the class, I want you to write up an essay about the cost of parenthood. Did you know it costs at least one hundred thirty thousand dollars to raise a child? I want you all to write a paragraph describing your hopes and dreams for your children and include how expensive it will be. Second paragraph, describe how far you'll go to have your biological children."

A few snickers throughout the room. Kenzie leans forward and whispers, "We're going to adopt."

I shake my head and whisper back. "Nope, we are going to try over and over and over until we are successful."

She smacks me on the back of the head.

"Settle down. For the third paragraph, describe how your life will be different if you do not or are not able to have children."

Multiple groans erupt throughout the class, but eventually, everyone settles down to do their work. I can only imagine what Kenzie is writing. I know I want my kids to reach for the moon but understand having a father that is a baker won't make it easy for them. They will have to work hard to obtain their own goals. I guess a baker wouldn't be able to adopt or do IVF, so if we can't have kids the old-fashioned way, I guess we're screwed, pun intended. And life would be different and maybe a little less full without children, but it would allow us to focus on the business or charity work. Maybe even foster a child.

Kenzie taps me on the shoulder. "I added something about fostering a child if we couldn't have one. Does that sound okay?"

I turn around and raise my eyebrows. "Stop reading my mind."

She peeks over my shoulder to read my paper, and her jaw drops. "Oh my gosh. Are you reading my thoughts?"

"Oh, Kenz, I wish."

She sneers at me. "Right now. What am I thinking?"

I lean over until we are nose to nose. "Hmm. I think you are still a little jealous of my non-girlfriend."

She huffs. "That's silly. I was thinking about what Mom said this morning. Dad is coming over to dinner tonight, and they are going to reconcile. I just know it."

Hamilton groans from the next aisle. "Not going to happen, sis. I think you're better off being a little jealous of the non-girlfriend."

When I chuckle, Mr. Carter shushes me.

Kenzie leans up right next to my ear, sending warm fuzzies down my neck. "I'm not jealous."

"Are too."

Tiffany shushes us, which makes me laugh.

After class, I tell the rest of the bandmates about the gig, and they all seem stoked. Anne walks up, and Hamilton whispers, "Here comes your non-date."

"Shut up."

"Hey, guys," Anne says as she smiles at everyone. "Did David tell you the good news?"

"Yeah," Dylan says. "Real cool."

"It's a lot of fun, and I'll make fliers to hang up everywhere. I can't wait to hear you all play."

"We better head to class." I close my locker, and Anne and I walk down the hallway in the opposite direction of the guys. "Hey, Anne. About last night."

"It was nice hanging out with you."

"Yeah. Did you think it was a little awkward?"

She nods. "Totally, but that's how first dates are."

I stop walking, and she looks at me with confusion written over her face. "I think you're great, but I don't know if I'm feeling it."

Anne touches my shoulder. "I completely understand. I didn't feel anything either. But if it makes Kenzie all jealous, I'm all in."

I blink like an idiot. "What did you say?"

Like a deer in the headlights, she backs away. "Forget what I said."

"No, there's no forgetting. What did that mean?"

Anne scans the hallway and chews on her lip. "Okay, I'll tell you, but you have to promise not to beat him up."

"Who? What are you talking about?"

"Michael," she whispers. "He paid me to ask you out to make his sister jealous."

Oh no he didn't. My ears are on fire. "When I get my hands on him—"

"You promised."

"No, I didn't."

"But did it work?"

I throw my hands in the air. "I don't know. This is seriously messed up."

"I do like you. You're a great guy, but you're not my type."

"What?" I yell so loudly everyone in the hallway stops what they are doing to watch us.

She takes me by the arm and drags me into calculus class. "Let's talk about this later. We have a test to take."

Oh, that's just perfect. I won't need that scholarship because I'm going to flunk out of calculus. And I'm going to be one friend short when I get my hands on Michael. He has some serious explaining to do.

Chapter 27

Michael's phone buzzes the entire ride home from school. White knuckled, he continues to drive, both hands on the wheel.

"Do you want me to see who keeps texting you? It's probably Mollie."

"No. It can wait."

He's acting odd, even for Michael. He's all twitchy, and twice, he's hit the curb turning a corner. "What's up with you?"

"Nothing."

I stare ahead as he drives like a fourteen-year-old. "Tonight will be perfect. I know Dad and Mom are getting back together tonight. I just know it."

"No, they aren't."

I wag my finger under his nose. "You wait and see. I've heard Mom talking to Dad a few times this week, and they weren't arguing. She giggled a few times too. So it's on."

He pulls into our driveway and turns off the engine. "Kenzie, don't get your hopes up."

"I don't know why you are so against them reconciling." I slam the truck door extra hard for emphasis before I stomp up to the front door. A rumble of thunder hurries my steps.

When I open the front door, Mom rushes around the kitchen, preparing a meal. The smell of beef, carrots, and potatoes filters through the air. I knew it. She's making Dad's favorite meal.

"Hey, Mom. Do you need any help?"

She smiles before motioning toward the cabinet. "You can set the table for me."

I bounce over to where she stores the fine china and pull out four plates. As I lay them on the table, Mom says, "Honey, that's not enough. You need two more."

I swing around to look at Michael. "Did you invite someone to dinner?"

Leaning up against the door frame, he shakes his head.

"Mom, who did you invite?"

She stares at me like I'm the densest person on earth, and right now, I guess I am. "Collin and Ava?"

"What?" My voice is so screechy, Michael covers his ears.

Mom hands me the silverware and shoos me toward the table. "It's a surprise."

Another clap of thunder sends me skittering around, looking for the flashlight. "I don't like surprises any more than I like storms."

Michael steals a carrot and chomps down. "Prepare for both."

I stomp down the hall toward my room and slam the door behind me. For the next few hours, I hide in my room, and no one bothers me. Mom has some nerve to invite all these outsiders into our house tonight.

The all-too-familiar loud muffler of Dad's muscle car rumbles down the street. The rain starts to fall in sheets, and as I peek out my window, I catch Dad as he rushes around to the passenger door and helps someone out of the car. She has long legs and very high heels.

Dad pushes open the front door and escorts Ava, I assume, inside as a knock comes at my door, making me jump.

"Get your butt out here," Michael says.

I stomp to the door, and like a petulant child, swing it open and push past Michael to force myself down the hallway before I can talk myself out of it. Ava, standing in the middle of the living room, is all giggly as she wipes the rain off Dad's face. It's not fair, and I think it should be illegal that none of her makeup is smeared from the rain and not a strand of hair is out of place.

Mom hugs Ava, and my head feels like it's about to explode. I keep pinching my arm to wake me up from this terrible dream.

"Ava, have a seat in the living room while I check on the pot roast." She motions for everyone to enter the living room, but I stand frozen in place. Mom takes me by the shoulders, turns me around, and gives me a nudge toward the little group meeting. "Ed, go ahead. Tell them."

Michael stands behind me and rests his hands on my shoulders.

Dad claps his hands together and clears his throat. A lightning flash overhead causes us all to jump. "I wanted you kids to know I love you very much."

Sure, you do.

"I wanted to share with you a few really big pieces of news."

He holds out two envelopes, giving me one and Michael the other. "Kenzie, open yours first."

I tear into it and read the words. I suck in a breath, and nothing leaves my lungs. "You're moving?"

Dad nods. "Yeah. I got a great job offer in Chicago. It's too good to pass up. And it's near Ava's parents."

The paper drifts out of my hand toward the floor, along with my hopes. Dad's leaving.

Michael rips into his envelope. "I hope this is round trip tickets to the Windy City."

Dad laughs. "No, but that's a given. You're always welcome to visit."

I slump into the seat next to me, watching the room spin as Michael slips a black-and-white photo from his envelope and turns it around for me to see the "It's a girl" caption above a sonogram photo. His face brightens as he says, "Well, what do you know, Kenz, we're going to have a baby sister."

Mom squeals and rushes toward Ava and embraces her. "Oh, I'm so happy for you."

Michael slaps Dad on the back as they continue babbling on about babies and Chicago. My head is buzzing.

Right when I think I'm going to throw up, I yell, "No!"

Everyone stops to stare at me.

I pace the living room. "This is not what was supposed to happen." I point to Mom and Dad. "You two were supposed to get back together." I steel my eyes on Ava. "And you were supposed to go find someone your own age."

"Kenzie." Dad jerks me around, stopping my pacing. "Apologize to Ava. We are in love, and we're getting married."

I shake my head, making all my brain cells slosh together. "No. You're still married to Mom, and you're going to get back together like you're supposed to." Tears well up in my eyes, and I yank my arm away from Dad's grip. "This can't be happening." I cover my face with my hands, and the tears stream down my face.

"Honey," Mom says, doing her best to console me. "Ed brought the divorce papers. I'm signing them tonight. I should have done this months ago. Leave it to me to procrastinate, but it's the right thing to do. I'm happy for him."

"Don't you still love him?" I glance at my mom, hoping there is the slightest trace of feelings left for my father.

She smiles at him, but it's one of those pity smiles. "I will always care for him, but we don't want to be married anymore. It's not a good match. None of this will change how he feels about you and Michael."

Dad rubs my back, and I jerk away as if his touch was as powerful as the lightning outside.

"Don't touch me."

I storm away from them, toward the front door.

"Kenzie, don't leave like this," Mom pleads, but I don't care.

Without a plan, I rush outside into the pouring rain. It fits how I feel right now. I am so lost. Nothing makes sense anymore.

AFTER TEN MINUTES OF standing outside David's bedroom window in the pouring rain, I finally muster enough courage to get his attention. Like we used to do when we were all friends, I tap on his bedroom window: tap, tap-tap, tap-tap-tap. All it takes is two seconds before his window scrapes open and a muscular arm reaches down for me to grab. He waves it in front of my face, but all I can do is stare at it. I'm not sure what my problem is. He's been really nice and super patient during this stupid project. I've been nothing but a jerk to him, but he smiles and takes everything I throw his way. And now I stand outside his window, wondering if I should accept a hand.

I've made it all the way across the street away from the drama I left in my wake, and now I am about to chicken out. Grabbing his hand should be the easy part. It would be out of the rain and away from the craziness full of hideous colors.

He waves his hand in front of me again to gain my attention, but all I can do is stare at it.

Come on, Kenzie, get a grip, and grab on to that hand. It's the lifeline you need.

But if I take his hand, it breaks down one more barrier before my world crumbles around me. I will have to admit I need help because everyone keeps letting me down. I'm setting myself up to have David let me down also.

He snaps his fingers, bringing me back to my sucky reality. And before I can talk myself out of it, I latch on to his strong hand, and the muscles in his forearm flex as he wraps his fingers around mine. With one quick motion, he yanks me up to the windowsill, and on autopilot, I throw my other hand up to grab his bicep.

David snatches me through the window like I am as light as his book bag. I crash into a wall of muscle fibers under his T-shirt that I didn't realize existed. His hands find my waist to steady me as I stand there, dripping water all over his hardwood floor. I wipe rain off my face and force an inch of distance between us. His laughter rumbles through his chest.

"What's so funny?"

"Nothing. I was just thinking about the last time I dragged you through the window. We were about the same size. I almost pulled my back out getting you up to my room, but I wasn't ever going to let you know about it."

A gasp escapes my mouth before I can stop it. "Are you saying I was fat?"

He backs up, taking in my soggy appearance. "Not at all, Kenz." He tosses me a sweatshirt, which takes me zero seconds to throw over my head. "I'm saying I was scrawny."

"Not anymore." I slap a hand over my mouth. I really need to apply a filter between my brain and my mouth.

Another rumble of laughter fills his room. While he mops up the rainwater with a T-shirt he left lying around, I stare at his back muscles flexing with every stroke. I know I should keep David in the ugly, "do not trust" column, but in the past month, he's shown me the side of him that I remember from childhood. He's quick with a smile, kind to everyone including me, and super sweet. And when I take my blinders off, I see what all the other girls see too. He's beautiful, regardless of his name.

He looks up at me, and our eyes meet. His brow scrunches together. "I'll take it this visit doesn't have anything to do with our project. But I do have the next assignment finished."

My lip trembles as I toe out of my sneakers. "No. It's not about the project. I need... I need someone, I need..."

He stops his cleanup and takes a step closer to me, so close, I can still smell the chicken he had for dinner. "You need... me?"

A tear slides down my cheek, merging with the raindrops. One octave above a whisper, I reply, "Yeah, maybe."

Another step, and he's so close, we share breaths. He tips my chin up with the slightest touch from his index finger. The connection sends tingles through my nervous system.

"Kenz, please talk to me. I'm here for you."

A tsunami of tears slides down my face, and I bury it in his chest. His warm arms wrap me in a human blanket of comfort as I sob, soaking his Twenty-One Pilots T-shirt. He doesn't say a word. In silence, he holds me like my body won't support its weight, which I don't think it can. With one hand planted firmly on the small of my back, he draws circles behind my neck with the other, then he runs his fingers through my tangled, wet hair. I'm pretty sure his lips grazed my forehead.

"Kenzie, breathe, or I might have to give you mouth-to-mouth. Not that I'm complaining, mind you."

I snort through my sobs.

"That's better." He releases me and sits on his bed. The mattress sags with his weight. He pats the empty space next to him, inviting me to sit. Before I take his offer, I take a deep breath and wipe my snotty nose on the sleeve of his sweatshirt, a surefire way to maintain ownership of it. I clear my throat and look into his bright eyes.

"Dad stopped by."

He nods. "I thought I heard his car. Is everything all right?"

I shrug as I collapse onto his bed beside him. "For him, it's awesome." I tuck my knees under my chin and pick at the hem of my skirt. "He came to tell me and Michael that he's moving to Chicago."

David grimaces.

"With his soon-to-be wife, Ava." My voice quivers. "Ava. Can you believe it?"

David puts a hand on my back, and the tears pick back up. I fall into his waiting arms and sob. "She's pregnant." I barely hear the growl in his chest from my moans.

The next thing I know, David scoops me up into his arms and, with the gentleness only he can show, then lays me down on his bed. He rests beside me with his arms wrapped around me. He kisses my temple and whispers, "Everything is going to be all right."

His sweet-as-cane-sugar voice flows over me, relaxing every tense muscle, so much so that I close my eyes. The last I hear is him saying, "I'll never leave you."

I want to believe him, but every person with ugly colors disappoints me. Soon enough, he will too. But for right now, I need the comfort he's so willing to give me, and I'm too exhausted to fight it.

Chapter 28

It's not that I hate the way Kenzie snuggles into me because it's pretty awesome. I'm kind of freaking out because I never expected her to come climbing through my window. But when I heard the familiar rumble from her dad's muffler, I knew something was about to go down.

As I watched from my bedroom window, I saw him slide his arm around his new woman, or more like his new girl, because she can't be more than five years out of college. But when he led her into Kenzie's house, not even bothering to knock, I wanted to punch something. That's not his house anymore. He had some nerve. I knew he was up to something, and even through the pelting rain, Kenzie's frantic voice spread right over the street.

It took every ounce of my willpower to not run over there and comfort her, and when I saw her scamper across the street and stand in the pouring rain under my window for the longest time, I didn't think my heart could beat any faster. Those ten minutes of her standing there getting drenched felt like an eternity.

When she tapped our secret code on my widow, I could finally breathe again. I almost didn't let her finish the third tap before I yanked the window open and grabbed that familiar hand. Now, as I lie on my bed with Kenzie snuggled up beside me asleep, my right arm is numb from the weight of her head on my shoulder, but there is no way in this lifetime I want her to move. The selfish me wishes she could stay in my room all night long, but the right thing to do is to let Hamilton know where she is. He must be worried.

I slip my phone out of my back pocket with my left hand and send a one-handed text message to her brother.

Me: *Kenzie's asleep in my bed.*

Hamilton: *???*

That sounded better in my head.

Me: *She cried herself to sleep.*

Hamilton: *You have that effect on girls.*

Me: *Shut up. Climb through the window.*

To avoid a punch in the jaw, I slide my numb arm out from under Kenzie and stand with no time to spare. When Hamilton taps, I open the window. Thank goodness I don't have to haul his sorry butt up because he weighs significantly more than she does. He falls to the floor with a thud.

"Shush." I point to Kenzie. The pins and needle sensation takes over my arm. "Crap, that hurts." I squeeze my fist to promote circulation.

"What's wrong with your hand?"

"Nothing. Kenzie's a mess about your dad."

Hamilton slides a hand through his wet hair. "I knew she wasn't going to take it well. That's why I suggested Dad tell her in person. I never thought he'd bring Ava with him. That was a dick move."

With all the force I can muster using only one un-numb arm, I shove him against the wall with a thud. "You want to explain anything to me?"

A sheepish grin slides across his face. "I don't know what you—" I force my forearm over his chest as he tries to suck in a breath. "Okay." When I back away, he sucks in a deep breath.

"You paid Anne to ask me out? Am I that hideous?"

Hamilton holds his hands out, and in a whisper, he says, "No, but I thought she needed some incentive." He points to his sister. "And it worked."

I take a step closer to him and poke him in the chest. "I'll deal with you later." I lean down toward Kenzie and slide a stand of hair off her face. "She's messed up bad. Bad enough to come to me for comfort." I give him a wry smile, but it's not genuine, and I should know better than to pull that on him.

He pats my back as he sits on the side of the bed. "Kenzie, wake up."

Her eyes flutter but don't open. She flops over to her other side. Hamilton looks up at me and says, "You try."

I lean over and whisper in her ear. "Wakey, wakey, sleeping beauty."

"Do I have to?"

Hamilton and I laugh at her. "Yeah. Sorry."

After a long groan, she yawns then opens her eyes. "How long was I out?" She snaps to a sitting position. "Where am I?"

Hamilton points at me. "You're in his bed, and I don't want to know the details."

She smacks him on the arm, then glances my way. "Stop it."

I gasp. "Stop what?"

She points to my face. "Those smiley eyes. Just stop it."

My mouth drops open. "I'm not sure what you mean."

She pokes me in the chest as she rises from the bed. "You know exactly what I mean. Like something scandalous happened."

Hamilton groans. "Kenz, stop it. You came to him, remember? So, for once, play nice with him."

Her expression changes from contrite to apologetic. "Sorry. I really needed someone to talk to."

I take a step toward her and rest my hands on her shoulders. "I will always be that someone for you."

She swallows hard. "I know. I'm so confused right now."

Hamilton clears his throat. "We need to go home and call Dad. Bitch him out if you want to, but it's not going to change anything."

She turns to her brother, and with a quivery voice, she says, "I don't know if I can. It's one more person that has let me down."

I lean down and whisper in her ear. "I'll never let you down."

"Eventually you will. It's inevitable."

Hamilton checks his phone. "We need to go."

"Yeah," she says in a whispered tone.

Right before Hamilton slips her through the window, she swivels around to face me. Her chest rises and falls with her rapid breaths. Breaking out of her trance, she rushes back to me, placing a hand on each side of my face. She pulls my head down toward hers until our mouths crash together. She deepens the kiss. I've wanted this for so long, but I'm not sure if she's kissing me because she wants to or if she's just overwhelmed. Either way, I'll take it. I snake my arms around her waist and hold her as tight as I can without crushing her ribs while a flash of purple spreads through my brain. Our lips separate, and we are nose-to-nose, both of us breathing erratically. *Did she see that too?*

Hamilton clears his throat. "We've got to go."

I've never wanted to throw a brick at my best friend more than I do right now. But even his insistence doesn't pop the bubble Kenzie and I are in. She touches my cheek and stares into my eyes. She flings her arms around my neck again and gives me another tight squeeze. I don't care if my right arm is only half working, I wrap her in the tightest embrace I can without bruising something. I sneak in a feather-light kiss on her cheek and another one on the side of her yummy lips before her brother breaks our connection and drags her out the window.

I could kiss her all day long if she'd let me. After today, maybe she won't detest me anymore. I hope this is a turning point for us and our project. It shows that in times of trouble, we get closer. We are a team during the good and the bad. It may suck about her father, but it's pretty much the best day ever as far as I'm concerned.

Chapter 29

I kissed David last night, and I liked it. A lot. I hope it wasn't a pity kiss, because I want more of that mouth on mine. I don't know what my problem has been all these years. He's pretty much the total package living right across the street from me, and I've done everything in my power to push him away, all because of my stupid color system.

I need to throw that whole theory out the window because no one is following the rules anymore. Dad and Mom were supposed to be compatible according to their colors, and they made it abundantly clear last night that they are moving on with their lives separately and are both happy for each other. Then David has been my friend all along and could be more than that if I could let everything go, let things happen naturally.

During the drive to school, my mind keeps reliving everything that happened last night: Mom's happiness for Dad's news, my total meltdown, my unlikely savior and his awesome lips. It was definitely a night for the books. And I'm going to pay for it today because I got absolutely no sleep.

When I walk down the hall toward first period, I notice David digging something out of his locker. The closer I get, the more nervous I become. My hands shake because I hope he didn't kiss me back only because he thought I needed it last night.

With a shy smile, he says, "Morning."

"Hey." I lean up against the locker next to his. "I'm sorry about last night."

His grin fades. "Oh."

He turns to leave, but I pull him back toward me. "I mean, I'm sorry I was a mess. I'm not sorry about the kiss. But if you didn't mean anything by it other than to comfort me, I totally get it. I know you like Anne, and that's your call, but that kiss was something else."

David places a finger to my lips to stop my rambling. He runs his finger down my cheek then lifts my chin and plants another soft kiss on my lips. My knees buckle, and I latch on to his bicep to keep from hitting the ground.

"Does that answer your question?"

I nod because I can't speak. After one more quick peck on the lips, he takes me by the hand and leads me into our class. When Tiffany sees our intertwined hands, she shrieks.

"Oh, my gosh. No. This cannot be happening."

David plants a kiss on the back of my hand, sending Tiffany into a fit of gags. As we take our place in the classroom, Michael fist-bumps David. I know Mr. Carter gave us another assignment, but I hear nothing. All I can do is focus on David's gorgeous head of hair right in front of me and count the minutes until I get to run my hands through it.

David turns around to me. "Do you want to work together on this assignment or alone?"

I blink. "What?"

He chuckles. "We're supposed to work on the form about behaviors in our marriage partner."

"Oh. Let's do it together."

David scoots his desk next to mine and leans close so our arms are touching. "I was hoping you'd say that. We're supposed to decide how bothered we would be if our spouse did the following things. First. How bothered would you be if I forgot your birthday?"

"Very bothered. You?"

He shrugs. "Somewhat bothered. How about if I put on weight?"

I shake my head. "Not bothered. You?"

He cringes, and I go in for a pinch when he says, "I'm kidding. I probably wouldn't even notice."

"Good answer." I scan the paper, and my eyes immediately go to question number nine. "What if your spouse had very little interest in sex?"

His eyes twinkle, and if we weren't surrounded by twenty classmates and a teacher, I would grab his face and make out with him right now. "That would bother me a lot because that's pretty much all us guys think about."

"Even if I gain weight?"

He inches closer and whispers, "Like I said, I wouldn't notice."

"Guys, stop with the mushy stuff," Michael says.

I crumple up a scrap piece of paper and throw it at him.

"Maybe we should finish this on our own."

David focuses on my lips and replies, "Probably a good idea."

It's not any easier doing this by myself because he doesn't move his desk, so his arm brushes up against mine with every stroke of his pen. Every time I sneak a peek over to him, I catch him doing the same thing. After his eyes dart away from me, I continue to stare at him, this time to see how long it will be before he glances back at me. It doesn't take thirty seconds, and as soon as he finds me still staring at me, he busts out laughing.

Mr. Carter stands up. "Okay, I see this isn't going as planned. How many people would bring me cookies if I said your projects could be presented on Monday and get this over with?"

Twenty hands rise in the air. I guess we're all ready to finish this project and get back to doing nothing in this period.

"Okay, get your projects ready. Check the rubric on how you'll be graded, and prepare to present. I'm going to go easy on you guys. The presentation isn't required anymore."

The class erupts in cheers, but Mr. Carter shushes us.

"Instead, each couple that prepares a five- to ten-minute presentation along with turning in all the assignments will receive extra credit. How does that sound?"

A collective sigh rushes through the class as the bell rings. Besides Mollie, I bet I'm the only other one that will try for the extra credit.

"Now get out of here before I change my mind."

I have never seen kids run out of a room so fast. The only ones left are me and David.

He takes me by the hand and walks me to my second-period class. "I haven't wanted to ask, but I do want to know how you're doing. Have you spoken to your dad?"

My shoulders slump, and I lean into him for support. "Not yet, but I will after school. I have to, even if I would rather watch my baby sister be born."

He trembles, making me laugh. "I know it's not ideal, and it's definitely not what you wanted, but if your parents are happy, try to be happy for them."

Barely above a whisper, I reply, "You're right. It's just so hard."

At the door to my second-period class, he pulls me into a hug, and I wish I could stay snuggled up against his muscular chest all day long. "At least you have both your parents. Be thankful for the little things."

I pull back and realize how selfish I sound. Here is a guy who didn't have any choice in the matter. His mother died, leaving his father a shell of the man he used to be. She left a little girl not knowing much about her mother and a son who had to grow up too quickly. I think they would all prefer to have Mrs. Shaw alive and living in a different house than not being around at all.

"I'm thankful for you." I pull his face down to mine and plant a quick peck on his lips.

Anne walks up and smiles. "You two are so cute together."

David looks like he could spit nails. "Thanks."

"Anne, I'm sorry if I swooped in and—"

"What? God no."

I stare from Anne to David. "I'm confused."

David points to Michael, who is lollygagging down the hallway until he sees us. He skids to a halt and backpedals.

"He... nothing. Anne and I, we, uh... it didn't work out."

"Oh."

Anne nods. "Yeah. Didn't work out. All is good, right?"

Something stinks, but I can't put my finger on it. David's molars are about to be ground to pulp, and Anne paints on a smile so fake a blind man could see it.

"Okay."

Anne turns on a dime and rushes away.

"That's so odd."

David blows out a breath and runs a hand through his hair. "You have no idea."

"See you later?"

His grin makes me weak in the knees. "You bet."

When I get home, Michael and I are going to have a twin talk to explain this very odd conversation. He's involved in some way, and I'll get to the bottom of it one way or another.

WAITING ON MICHAEL at his truck, I know the second he sees me because he freezes. I motion with one finger for him to approach, which he does at a snail's pace.

"You want to explain the hallway awkwardness?"

He gives me a one-shoulder shrug. "David was trying to make me jealous. He knows I have a thing for Anne."

I plant my hands on my hips as he takes one tentative step at a time until he's at his car. "Since when?"

He rolls his eyes. "Pfft. Since forever. Do you think it worked?"

The thought of Mollie's heart being ripped into shreds has me thinking of new and improved ways to destroy his family jewels.

"And hurt Mollie? You know the right thing to do would be for me to send a photo of you being potty-trained to everyone at school, right?"

He cocks his head to the side and grins. "Except all those pictures of me include you sitting on your potty right next to me."

I scowl at him. "Phooey."

"Come to think of it, I don't think Anne is right for me."

"Duh. If you hurt my best friend, I will disown you."

"Yes, ma'am. So, you and David. It's about time."

When I grab him around the waist to hug him, he lets out a huge sigh. He wraps his hands around my shoulders and squeezes the life out of me. "It was hard being the middleman."

"I know. I'm hoping I can be more open-minded and let my heart figure out what's good for me."

He pulls away from me and checks my forehead with his hand. "Are you sick or something? You must not be my sister. My sister lets color combinations dictate her every like and dislike."

I shove him away from me and march to the passenger door. "Hush. I'm trying not to be that girl anymore."

"Good, because she was a weirdo for sure."

While we drive home, I pull out my phone and call Dad. I might as well get this over with. "Hey, Dad, it's Kenzie. I'm sorry about last night."

"Me, too, sweetie. I never want to hurt you."

After letting out a deep breath, I continue. "I know that. I want you to be happy. If Mom is okay with everything, I guess I should be too."

"You mean it?"

"Yeah." *Do I?*

"Oh, Kenzie, you have no idea how much that means to me to hear you say that. I didn't get any sleep last night worrying about you." The relief plays through my phone.

I hold the phone out to Michael. He talks into the speaker. "Hey, Dad. She's not lying. I think she's actually happy for you." After I punch him on the arm, he adds, "Ow. Okay, I know she is. We'll come visit you after you get settled in Chicago."

"I would love that. Kenz, are you going to be okay with Ava? I don't want any trouble. I know you think she's young, but she's only five years younger than your mother."

Michael and I share a look. "Dad, I can't say that I'll see her like you do, but I will try to get along with her for your sake."

"And your baby sister's. Ava wants you to name her."

My breath hitches, and I can hardly breathe, let alone form words.

Michael laughs. "I think she's happy about that."

"Yeah." It's all I can squeak out.

"I love you two so much. See you soon."

"Bye, Dad," Michael says. When I disconnect the phone, Michael gives me an I-told-you-so expression. "That wasn't so hard, now was it?"

"It was very hard, but I'm trying."

He ruffles my hair, and I swat his hand away. "You are such a weird little sister. I am so glad there will be another Hamilton sister soon so I won't be stuck with just the likes of you."

I snort. "Sorry, bud. You're forever stuck with me. The good, the bad, and the ugly."

Michael mulls over my words. "Just try to do more good than bad, and you can't do much about the ugly."

I gasp and smack him on the arm. "I'm going to tell Mollie how evil you are, and she'll change her tune about you."

With a wide grin, he says, "Too late. She is officially my girlfriend, and it feels pretty freakin' lit."

My excitement spills over in my seat as I bounce around, hardly able to contain myself. "Mollie and I have a lot to talk about."

"As long as you leave potty-training photos out of the conversation, I think we'll be good."

I hold out my pinkie for him to wrap his around. "Pinkie promise. No incriminating photos."

For the first time since Mom and Dad split up, I feel as light as air. Things are clicking into place. Mom has Collin, who is ugly, but she seems to like him, and he adores her. Plus, he likes *The Princess Bride*. Dad has Ava and a new baby on the way. Michael has finally admitted he likes Mollie, and I have feelings for David. Things are looking up. I can't imagine anything happening to mess up this frame of mind.

Chapter 30

Never in a million years did I think I would be walking down the street of our neighborhood, hand in hand with Kenzie. She and Fiona chatter on and on about *Prince Not-So-Charming* and if Christopher Hines and Alyssa Green are a couple in real life. Catarina tugs on the leash for us to walk faster, but I don't want this day to end. This is what I've wanted for so long.

"What do you think?" Fiona bounces beside me, causing Catarina to pick up her pace.

"Uh... I wasn't paying attention."

Kenzie bumps my hip with hers. "She wanted to know if Gus should have tried out for the baseball team or joined the debate club." She then mouths "both" to give me the answer Fi wants to hear.

"I think the wise move would be to choose both."

Fiona beams. "And he gets to spend the most time with Catarina."

I gaze over at Kenzie, and my gut twists. Our time barely has gotten started, and it could end way too soon. We've never had the college talk before because, until now, it didn't matter. But I have no idea what her plans are. With my luck, she'll go across the country and find some hot, smart dude and forget all about me.

"As much time as possible is a good thing. Don't you think, Kenz?"

She wraps her arms around my waist and gives me a big squeeze. My heart flutters with every touch. I never want this day to end unless I know there will be another one just like it tomorrow. "A very good thing. Fiona, where should I go to college?"

My eyebrows shoot up. Her mind-reading skills must be kicking into overdrive today. I better mute my brain before she understands more of my thoughts.

Fiona looks up at the sky. "Well, you probably want to go somewhere away from here, unless you want to be close to David."

Kenzie looks up at me and shrugs. That gives me no indication of what her intention is. "If your brother wants that scholarship, I think we should look at his website one more time before he submits it."

"Can I hit the Submit button?" Fiona runs around me and Kenzie with Catarina barking at her heels.

"Sure. Let's do that right now," I say.

"Yes!" Kenzie squeals and kisses me on the cheek. This is a far cry from her throwing daggers my way.

As we walk back to my house, Fiona keeps staring at Mom's rings on Kenzie's finger.

"Kenzie, are you two really going to get married now?"

Kenzie looks like she swallowed a bug, and I wish I could find a sinkhole to swallow me whole. She opens her mouth to speak, but nothing comes out.

"Fi." I poke her in the belly. "You do realize we are still teenagers, right? Got a lot of living to do before either of us is at the marrying stage."

My sister's face falls, and she kicks a small rock out of her path. I know Fiona cares for Kenzie almost as much as I do, but in no way am I going to scare Kenzie off with such talk as that.

"Does that mean you'll have to give back Mama's rings?"

Kenzie gazes down at her left hand. The diamonds twinkle in the setting sun. "Yes. This was for a school project. These are for you someday. I'd never take anything that belongs to you."

My throat clogs thinking of my mother. I still remember the day she took the rings off her finger and forced my father to put them in the storage box. I think he cried as much that day as the one when she died. She refused to be buried with them because she wanted either me or Fiona to have them as a reminder of the strong bond she had with our father.

"You all right?" Kenzie asks in a soft, soothing voice.

I nod. It's like I've missed a key component of my life for so many years. And I guess I'll never get over losing my mother. Some days are easier to manage, but most days, it's a deep, dark void that I can never get past.

When we climb the steps to my house, Catarina makes a beeline to her water bowl. Fiona runs to my bedroom and brings my laptop into the kitchen.

"Hope you don't have any nudie pictures on here because I will be seriously grossed out if you do."

"None, I promise."

Kenzie giggles. "Let's hope they don't show up on the website again."

Fiona's eyes bug out of their sockets, and I give Kenzie a stare, hoping she can read my mind to not say those kinds of things in front of my little sister.

I log on to the laptop and let Kenzie do the honors of pulling up the website. When she lets out a big sigh, I assume it's safe for young eyes to see.

"It's perfect." She turns it around and shows me the site.

Kenzie even added the small concert at Pizza Perfect scheduled for next week. And like she said, the website is awesome. It's simple but fun, and I am pretty sure I can manage the site with updates whenever possible. In another tab, I open the Bellevue University scholarship page, which I have bookmarked, my partially completed application at the ready.

With my two favorite girls by my side, I drag and drop the website URL into the space provided. I scan the form one more time for accuracy before I step out of the way for Fiona to take over command of the laptop.

"Okay, kiddo, click away."

"Drum roll." Kenzie plays a riff on the table with her fingers.

Fiona clicks the Submit button, and when the laptop bings, we know it's been sent. We high-five each other.

Then Fiona asks, "Does this mean you got the scholarship?"

"I wish. It means they received my application. The deadline is next week, and they will decide in about a month."

She rolls her eyes and scoops up Catarina. "That stinks. Oh well, we're going to watch a movie."

"Hey, Fi, I'll bring you some bread if I make a loaf."

"Yes!" she yells after she's already left the room.

Kenzie giggles. "Love that kid."

"Me too."

I slide my arms around her waist, and she comes to me willingly. When she slips her arms around my neck, my heart skips a beat. My forehead rests on hers, and we breathe the same air.

"I can't thank you enough. This means the world to me," I say.

"I know it does."

After giving her a quick kiss, I pull back. "I guess this means you're done working with me. We had a deal."

She shoves me on the shoulder. "Yeah, I guess we did. Lucky for me, the project is almost over anyway."

"So, does that mean...?"

Kenzie bats her eyes in an exaggerated fashion. "I don't know, Mr. Shaw. Maybe if you behave, I'll stick around a little longer."

Like a predator on its prey, I pin her up against the kitchen counter. "Is this behaving?" I give her a scorching-hot kiss, and by the way her knees buckle, I'm pretty sure I know the answer.

Someone clears their throat. I whip my head around to find Dad standing there, one eyebrow cocked.

"Hey, Dad. We were just celebrating me submitting the application for that scholarship I was telling you about."

He opens the refrigerator door and pulls out a Coke bottle. "Good thing Fiona didn't witness the celebratory actions."

Kenzie's face flushes bright red, and she slides a strand of hair behind her ear. "Hi, Mr. Shaw. I was just leaving." She waves to me as she slips past Dad and out the door, my gaze fixed on her the entire time.

"That's a complete one-eighty, don't you think?"

I shrug. "Yeah."

He leans against the counter and takes a swig from his bottle, then scratches his head. "Don't get me wrong, I think the world of Mackenzie, but it seemed like she hated your guts just last week."

I let out a chuckle. "That is pretty accurate."

"And now?"

I throw up my hands. "Now, she likes me. I'm trying not to psychoanalyze it. I just want to enjoy it."

Dad chokes on his Coke. "Oh, I think you were enjoying it all right, right in my kitchen."

"Dad..."

"So, did she talk to you about why she was so grumpy for so long?"

I shake my head. "I didn't ask. Like a switch, things changed for her, and I like it this way."

He stares at the ceiling as if the spackling will give him the words he's searching for. "And you're sure she won't switch back just as fast?"

I cross my arms over my chest. "What's that supposed to mean?"

He throws his hands out in defense. "Nothing except I know how you've always felt about her. I don't want you to get hurt if she plans on going back to not talking to you again. You've had enough women leave you."

Dad doesn't have the right to compare Mom dying to Kenzie changing her mind about me. "I don't know why she didn't like me for all those years, but she does now. Whether it lasts two weeks or two decades, I don't care right now."

"Okay." He peeks down the hallway before adding, "Just keep it PG around Fiona, and stay out of your bedroom."

Heat soars up my neck, and if my ears are as red as they feel, I should have flames coming out of them. "Dad, I know the rules."

He pops me on the shoulder. "It's my job to remind you of the rules, and I get to pick the number of reminders I give out, so it won't be the last."

"Thanks for the warning."

He takes a deep breath and chuckles. "Good luck with the scholarship."

My mouth splits into a huge grin. "Thanks. I think I have a good shot at it. I'll know in about a month."

He nods. "You deserve it. And if you don't get it, we'll think of something. We always do."

Dad lets out a yawn as he meanders down the hallway. Catarina lets out a chirpy welcome-home bark and runs circles around him in the hallway, making him stumble to keep from squashing her. I hate that Dad put a seed of doubt in my brain because I really don't care about the past. It doesn't matter why she hated me so much. She doesn't now. That's all that matters.

Chapter 31

It's a little awkward sitting around our dinner table, working on the finishing touches to our project. Every chance I get, I extend my leg to touch David's, and each time, his face turns flaming red. Mollie gushes with excitement. She and Michael couldn't be any cuter. Thank goodness the project got them stuck together because I think both of them were too darn shy to make the first move. And I'm so glad he didn't go for Anne.

David keeps glaring at Michael for some crazy reason. They usually get along so great, as if they are the twins in the room, but today, David seems agitated with him. Mollie chatters constantly, and Michael laughs at appropriate times, but I don't think any of us are listening to a word she says.

Michael says, "I think we have a good setlist for the Pizza Perfect crowd. Mollie offered to put up signs everywhere, and I posted it on social media, so we might have a decent showing."

David nods. "Yeah, I'll tell Anne what to expect."

Michael chokes on his Sprite. When he catches his breath, he says, "Yeah, you do that."

David lays down the poster board he's been working on and leans over the table. "I'm still ticked off about all of that."

"All of what?" Mollie and I ask at the same time.

David points at Michael then shakes his head. "Nothing."

I glance at Mollie. "We probably don't want to know."

Mollie rolls her eyes. "No doubt. Besides…" She gets an evil twinkle in her eye. "You owe me."

My brow scrunches up so much I'm going to have permanent wrinkles. "Huh?"

Her grin is huge, causing me to worry a bit. "Remember when you said this project would confirm what you already knew, and I would have to say, 'I told you so' if you were right?"

Uh-oh.

"And if you were wrong, which you *were* wrong, by the way, you would owe me."

Crap. I forgot all about that conversation. I stare at David, who looks as confused as I felt when she first spoke.

"Confirm what you already knew about what?" David cocks his head to the side.

Michael cheeses. "Yeah, sis. What?"

This is not the time, and I don't ever want to explain my color system to David because I was obviously way off. One day, I'll tell him, and maybe we'll get a big laugh out of it. But not today.

"Nothing." I turn to Mollie and take a deep breath. "What do I owe you?"

She stares at the ceiling until an evil grin plays across her face. "For your project presentation, you have to dress up as Miracle Max."

David and Michael high-five each other.

"What? Billy Crystal's character in *The Princess Bride*? The old dude that says, 'Have fun storming the castle' and 'mostly dead'?"

"Yep."

I shake my head until my eyeballs hurt. "Inconceivable. Why not Princess Buttercup? Even Prince Humperdinck would be a better choice."

All three of them shake their heads.

"Miracle Max." Mollie hugs me. "It's going to be epic."

Oh, it will be epic all right.

AFTER MOLLIE LEAVES, David and I sit on the porch in silence. I lean my head on his shoulder, and I mentally kick myself for wasting so much time being angry at this person for nothing important at all. It's such a relief just being myself and letting things happen the way they are supposed to. I didn't know how trapped I was making myself because of my stupid rules. It's scary, but I know I can trust myself now.

"What did Mollie mean by 'confirming what you already knew'?"

Mollie doesn't even really know about my color decisions, so I should have kept my mouth shut about that in the first place.

"Oh, nothing. I tend to decide how I feel about people and not change my mind." It's the truth, even if it's a completely watered-down version of the situation.

He plays with a strand of my hair, sliding it through his fingers. "Did you change your mind about me?"

"Yes."

"We used to be friends. What happened?"

This is the number one question I hoped he would never ask me. I don't have a logical answer for him, and my feeble attempt to describe what happened will make me sound odder than I already am.

"Can I just say I was an idiot and leave it at that?"

He takes my face in his hands and stares into my eyes. After a soft kiss on my mouth, he whispers, "Okay."

Dodged a bullet. "I cannot believe I have to dress up like Miracle Max."

He throws his head back and belts out a hearty laugh. "Can't wait. And you have to say, 'Truuuuuue looooovve' at the end. Promise?"

I roll my eyes. "Fine. I will never make a bet again."

"That's probably a good policy."

Catarina's barking from across the street gets our attention.

"I better go. Dad's going to be late coming home today, and if I'm not over there to partially oversee Fiona, she'll feed the dog Pop-Tarts."

Fiona waves to us as she plays with her dog in the front yard.

David stands and stretches, allowing his T-shirt to rise just enough for me to enjoy the view. He takes me by the hand to help me up and plants another kiss on my cheek. "See ya tomorrow."

"Bye, David."

His eyes get big. "You said my name."

I bite my lip to stop the smile from forming on my face. "I like your name now."

After another peck on the cheek, he replies, "You're so adorable."

I watch him gallop across the street, throw his sister over his shoulder like a sack of potatoes, and carry her inside. All the while, Catarina yips at their feet, and Fiona giggles constantly. They are so cute together.

A large burp comes from behind as Michael sits beside me, chomping down on an apple. After another swallow, he says, "You are going to make an awesome Miracle Max."

I bury my face in my hands. "Don't remind me."

"Does Mollie know about your color craziness? Because it kind of sounded like she did."

"No, thank goodness."

He throws the apple core into the bushes and wipes his sticky hands on my leg. *Ew.* "I'm glad the color-coding algorithm, whatever it was, is behind you. It was stupid. David is a good guy, like I said he was. Mom is happy with Collin. Dad is happy with Ava. I was right all the way around. Just let me make all your life decisions for you, and you'll be fine."

My eyes hurt from the eye roll I give him. "Whatever." After a long pause, I say, "I think you and Mollie are such a cute couple."

He blushes. "Yeah, well. I guess this project turned out pretty decent after all."

David waves to us from his front door, and we wave back. After a moment of silence, I rest my head on my brother's shoulder and let out a deep sigh. "It sure did."

Chapter 32

I'm as nervous as a fox at a hound convention. It's been a while since we performed anywhere except in Hamilton's garage. Now, tons of people from school say they are going to show up, but it's one cute brunette that has me sweating through my deodorant. She sits at the front table with Mollie, and they giggle like most girls do.

Anne walks out from the kitchen and freezes when she sees Kenzie. She backs up and heads to the cash register instead.

Kenzie scrunches her eyebrows together. "What's that all about?"

"Nothing."

She stares at her hands resting on the table and asks, "Are you sure?"

I lean down and kiss her cheek. "I'm positive."

Dylan clears his throat. "Dude, we need to warm up."

He lets out a riff, and while Anne rings up a customer's order, she says, "Wow, he is so cool."

Dylan stares a hole through her. "I'd rather be dead than cool."

She claps her hands over her mouth. "Oh my gosh. You're a Cobainian, aren't you?"

He whips his hair out of his face and flashes her a wicked grin.

Anne bounces behind the cash register. "I love Nirvana so much."

Mollie and Kenzie groan. To think there is a female person perfect for Dylan is a little creepy, to say the least. But it does give him a little boost to shred chords I've never heard from him before.

Anne's brother takes a microphone. "Hey, everyone. Thanks for coming to Tuesday Tunes at Pizza Perfect. Sit back, enjoy pizza, and get ready to rock out to Nash Trash."

Kenzie wolf whistles and blows me a kiss as the crowd claps for us. We start with a cover tune from Mumford & Sons, getting everyone warmed up. It doesn't take long before Kenzie stands and sways to the music. When I get to the line about being all I ever longed for, she grins, knowing I'm singing to her.

When the song is over and the small crowd goes crazy, I can finally breathe.

Kenzie mouths to me, "You are awesome."

I wink at her.

"Thanks. This next one is something I wrote. I hope you like it."

Dylan cuts loose on the entry.

For the next thirty minutes, we crank out the tunes, and when the hat is passed, we actually make a few bucks. As the crowd disperses and we pack our gear, Kenzie jumps on the small stage, snatches a set of drumsticks from Rhett, and plays a riff on the counter. He holds his hand out for his sticks, and she pouts but gives them back to him.

She turns to me and grins. "You were awesome."

I scan the small stage. "It was a group effort."

She shakes her head. "Your voice. It's very smooth. And sexy. Why haven't I noticed that before?"

My grin is going to break my face. "You must have high-quality noise-canceling headphones."

"I do, but no more. You are so good." She leans into me and gives me a quick peck on the cheek.

"Thank you for not hating me anymore."

Kenzie blinks and looks off for a moment, then says, "I never hated you. I just had a strange way of liking or not liking people."

I belt out a laugh and pull her into a hug. "You got the strange part right."

As I lean in for a kiss, Anne walks out from the kitchen with a huge grin. "You guys were great." She turns to Kenzie and, with a cringy expression, adds, "I'm so sorry. I hope I didn't make things awkward." She points to Hamilton. "He was afraid you wouldn't act without some prodding."

Kenzie stumbles backward, bumping into the drum kit. "What?"

Anne glances from me to Michael, and her cheeks turn red. "Um, I guess you didn't tell her?"

"Tell me what?" Kenzie asks through clenched teeth.

Hamilton jumps up and backs away from his feisty twin sister. "Now, sis. It was for your own good."

If Kenzie could emit fire from her eyes, I think it would be happening right now. "What. Did. You. Do?"

I plant a hand on each of her shoulders. "He thought you needed a nudge in my direction, so he created some competition. He... bribed Anne to ask me out to make you jealous."

She lunges forward, but I latch onto her waist in a tight grip. "Oh, he's going to get a nudge. That's for sure."

Mollie scoots out of the way, and I don't blame her. All this arm flailing Kenzie's doing might result in some unnecessary injuries.

From the other side of the stage, Michael says, "Kenzie, I didn't mean any harm, but I knew if you had a little competition, you might start to see David differently. And it worked, so yay you... and him." He holds his arms out as if he just won a competition.

I lean down and whisper, "Let it go. He meant well."

Michael laughs. "I also meant well when I messed with the website." He uses air quotes, and Kenzie sucks in all the oxygen in the room.

"What did you say?"

He rolls his eyes. "Sis, I knew you'd create that website in a single day, so I had to figure out a way to keep you two together for a little longer."

Kenzie stares at me. "Did you know about this?"

I back up and throw my hands up to defend myself from her wrath. "This is news to me too."

She pummels her brother on the shoulder with her fists as he backs away in a feeble attempt to get out of her way. "Stop. It worked, didn't it?"

"The boob pics? That was your doing?"

"Yep." He seems very proud of himself, and I'd like to be mad at him, but it's actually funny.

She whacks me in the stomach, extinguishing my chuckle. "That could have ruined your chances of getting the scholarship."

I stare at Hamilton and wait for his reaction. He sighs. "I wasn't going to let that happen. I knew he had plenty of time to submit the application. I may be devious, but I'm not evil."

Kenzie pokes Hamilton in the chest. "I cannot believe you sabotaged David's website I was building so I would have to spend more time with him."

Mollie giggles as she high-fives Hamilton. "I was wondering if you had something to do with that. I'm just sorry I didn't think of it first."

Kenzie gasps, but Mollie gives her shoulder a shove.

"You are a terrible best friend," Kenzie says.

I wrap my arm around Kenzie's shoulders. "It's all good now."

Kenzie sneers at her brother. "Is there anything else you want to get off your chest? Because confession seems to be good for your soul, brother."

Michael squeezes his eyes shut and spews from his mouth, "And I hacked into the server where Mr. Carter keeps his lesson plans and switched the partners for the project so you and David would be forced to work together." Michael immediately scoots away from Kenzie.

"You did what?" Her screechy voice cuts through the restaurant, turning a few heads.

"Like I said, it was for your own good. I figured you needed a lesson. There was only one way to show that your color system did or didn't work, and that was to conduct a blind experiment. And I was right. It didn't matter."

Color system?

She paces the stage as she cuts her eyes toward me. Her hands shake as she pokes Michael in the chest. "I cannot believe you did that. Do you know how hard it was to work with him at first?"

Ouch.

"Yes, but not anymore. You guys are stuck together like Elmer's glue. I'm starting to think I went overboard in my skills because it's pretty gross how much you are attached now. First you hate him. Now you can't keep your hands off him. You're like a freakin' roller coaster with your extreme emotions."

Kenzie juts her chin high, and her smirk is deadly. "Two can play this game. Mollie, did you know that when Michael was four, he taped his tee-tee to his leg because it kept standing up?"

My jaw drops, and on instinct, my hand covers my junk.

Mollie covers her face with her hand as Kenzie glares at her brother. Rhett drops his drumsticks, and Dylan buries his head in his sheet music. I hold my breath, waiting for the bomb to land on its intended target.

His chest rises and falls, and his face gets all splotchy. Hamilton goes from cringy to angry in about three seconds. "Look, Kenz. This could have all been avoided if you didn't rely on your stupid color theory to make all your decisions. Including if you could trust David."

Kenzie's spine stiffens. "Shut up."

The blood in my veins freezes, but my face is on fire.

Hamilton gets a wicked expression on his face as he says, "It's true." He turns to me. "Did you know she hasn't liked you for years because the letters in your name aren't pretty colors?"

"Michael, stop it," she grinds out through a clenched jaw.

"Excuse me?" The ground spins beneath my feet, and the frozen burrito I ate this afternoon is about to spew from my mouth. "Say again?"

With a shaky hand, he points to his sister. "Yeah, she sees letters and numbers in color, and only pretty color combinations work for her. That's why she had her schedule rearranged—because it wasn't a pretty color. That's also why she thinks Mom and Dad should have gotten back together."

"Michael, stop—"

"She didn't like you all these years because the D and the A and the V are ugly. It's seriously messed up."

Kenzie's face pales. All this time, I thought I had done something wrong. All these years, I've wracked my brain to find that one pivotal moment where I hurt her so much that she would instantly hate me. I thought it was me. And it wasn't me at all.

Kenzie holds her hands out in front of her. "I can explain."

I shake my head. "I don't think you can."

Kenzie takes a step toward me. "None of that matters anymore. I was wrong."

"No." My word stops her in her tracks. "I kept hoping one day you would forgive me for whatever I did to you, but that wasn't going to happen because I never did anything at all. Right?"

Kenzie's eyes well with tears. "It's complicated."

I stare at my friends in the restaurant. Mollie's face is as white as a sheet. Dylan and Rhett have mysteriously vanished. Hamilton trains his eyes on the ground. Tears trail down Kenzie's cheeks, but I don't care.

"I have to go," I say barely above a whisper.

"David, please—"

I throw my hand up to stop her begging. "I don't want to hear any more."

Kenzie's gaze darts to her brother then to me. "Sure, you'll listen to him but won't even give me a chance to defend myself."

A sarcastic snort spews from my mouth. "Riiiigght. Like you let me defend the stupid colors of my name?"

The volume of my words causes Kenzie to flinch. "You don't understand." Her lip trembles, but she nods as if she's having an internal monologue. With fire in her eyes, she stiffens her spine. "I knew this would happen. I always knew you would let me down, and here we are."

"Guess you were right." I glance around at my so-called friends. "I... I need some air." I turn my back to them and walk out of Pizza Perfect, toward my car.

What started as the perfect night ended on the sourest of notes, to say the least. I can't wrap my head around the truth bomb that blew up in my face tonight, and I've never felt so betrayed by Kenzie. I don't understand her stupid color theory, and I don't think I want to. It makes no sense, but neither does caring for someone who doesn't care back.

Chapter 33

Mollie holds me around the shoulders while Michael drives us back to our house. Tears block my vision, and my breath hitches so much I can't catch my breath.

"What am I going to do?" My breaths are ragged as I wipe my snotty nose on my sleeve.

The truck comes to a stop at our house, and I stumble up the driveway. When Michael opens the front door, my mother takes one look at me and rushes over. "What in the world?"

I fall into her arms and bawl. "It's awful, Mom."

She walks me over to the couch and holds me as I drench the front of her shirt with tears. Michael stands next to the front door, hands in his pockets, while Mollie sinks on the couch next to me.

"Kenzie, I'm sure it will be all right." Mom tugs on my chin, forcing me to look at her. "What happened?"

I point to Michael. "He ruined things between me and David."

Michael holds his hands out in front of him as he walks in front of the couch. "Okay, listen. Maybe I shouldn't have said that, but you can't pin this on me. You were the one with this stupid obsession with colors."

Mom scrunches up her brow. "I'm not following you."

As I hold Mom tighter, my disowned brother fills Mom in on the way I see letters and numbers, and how certain combinations are ugly. She cocks her head to the side. "Let me get this straight. You let the way a name looks determine if the person is good or bad, instead of investing the time to figure out if the individual is good or bad, right?"

I sniffle. "It's never let me down. The word David is..."

"Oh, my Lord. Is that why you have been so against him all these years?"

"Yes. The colors made it easy to figure out who could be trusted and who couldn't. But I decided I was wrong about it all and let David into my life again, but then Michael spilled the beans to him."

Mom processes my confession then says, "Sweetheart, it would have come out eventually, don't you think?"

I peer up at Michael and say, "Maybe. But he should have let me make that decision."

"True," Mom says as she brushes a strand of hair behind my ear. "I think it's time I tell you something that might make things easier for you to understand about your abilities."

Looking into her eyes, I ask, "What?"

"You are not alone in this. Your father tastes colors."

There is a collective gasp throughout the room. Maybe this synesthesia thing is genetic. It would explain a lot. It's not an excuse, but it would make sense as to where I got it.

Michael says, "No way."

Mom nods. "Yeah, I thought there was something wrong with him because he said he could taste a Peppermint Patty if he walked past one in a store. And words with 'eh' in them smelled like bacon." She waved her hand in the air. "I didn't get it."

My mouth drops open. "I get it completely."

She lets out a sigh. "He didn't let it get in the way of living. You have to let some things go. It's not the end of the world to dislike a color."

I cover my face with my hands. "I've messed this up so bad. I let one aspect of myself control my thoughts and feelings instead of allowing my heart to see what's been right in front of me all along. Not that it matters anymore. David hates me now."

Mollie rubs my back. "Do you blame him? He's cared about you for so long, and you would have nothing to do with him. He thought he did something wrong to make you hate him."

Michael leans against the wall and says, "I cannot count how many times he's gone on and on about what he possibly could have done to make you hate him. I've wanted to tell him a bunch of times, but I didn't want to make things worse."

Mollie gives him a knowing stare. "Well, *that* plan backfired, didn't it?"

Staring up at my brother, I ask, "Why did you have to say anything?"

"I wasn't thinking. I spewed something before I thought it through. You know how I am."

Mollie stands next to Michael. "You can't blame Michael. This is something you brought on yourself."

Mom sighs. "Mackenzie, do you like David? I mean really, really like David?"

"I do. I've fought it for so long, and I don't care how ugly he is."

Mollie holds up a finger. "Uh, have you looked at him lately? He's a babe. No offense, Michael."

He pulls Mollie tight against him. "None taken, my bride."

Mom shrugs. "You have to fix this. If you let him get away, I will figure out your color system and date every ugly-worded guy there is."

"Mom, Collin is not all that pretty."

She smiles. "Done. He's moving in, so the ugliness will be all around you."

Mom gives me another hug, and I stand to face my brother. It's not his fault, but it's much easier to blame someone else for my problems.

"Michael, I'm sorry for what I said too."

"What did *you* do?" Mom gives me the stink eye.

Michael snorts and says, "She countered with the penis-taping incident."

"You didn't." Mom covers her smile with a hand on her lips.

Cringing, I say, "Yeah. Not my finest moment. Sorry about that, bro."

He pulls the waistband of his jeans away from his body and peers inside. "It survived, so I guess if you can forgive me, I can forgive you."

"Deal."

Mollie and Michael surround me in a bear hug as another round of tears falls.

"I never meant for this to happen, and I never thought I would care so much about David." I take a deep breath and add, "I think I might love him."

Mollie steps back, her mouth hangs open. "Oh my gosh. That's inconceivable." Of course, she would quote *The Princess Bride*.

Maybe I should have kept that part to myself. But I feel something for him that I've never felt before. It's just as unexplainable as my color system, but with more gushy feelings. And I ruined it.

Michael's phone buzzes, and when he reads the text, his mouth turns down into a frown. "It's David. He wants me to tell you..." Michael stares at his phone then grimaces.

I grab it and read the text myself.

David: *Tell Kenzie I'll finish the project and presentation. And it won't hurt my feelings if she doesn't show up for class.*

I close my eyes and squeeze out more tears.

"I'm really sorry, Kenz," Michael says.

Mom shakes her head. "Now, I don't blame him in the least, but you have to get a grade for this project, too, so you will march your butt into that classroom and do your part. Do you understand me?"

I can't do that. He's so mad at me, there's no telling what he'll do. The project is ruined regardless of if I'm present or not. "I don't know,

Mom. I've never seen him this mad. He might pick me up and throw me through the window."

Michael laughs. "He may want to, but he wouldn't do that. It would only make Tiffany happy, so you have that going for you."

"Tif is going to have a field day with this. And it wouldn't surprise me if he would rather be with her than with me after the mess I made." I rub my temples. I'm a doofus, and I have to fix it. A splash of color runs through my mind, and the answer is glaringly obvious. "I know you two probably have to finish your projects, but I would love it if you could help me with mine. David can do his own thing, but I'm going to do one also, and it's going to fix everything."

Michael rubs his hands together. "Let's do this."

I've got a great idea for the project display. I know I'll get a good grade, but I hope I get more than that. It may be too much to ask for David's forgiveness. He may make me wait for years like I did him, and I would deserve it. My project is going to blow Mr. Carter's mind. And even if I don't get any sleep tonight, I have some serious baking to do. I need to pull out all the stops to get a good grade *and* win back my guy. If this doesn't work, I don't know what I'm going to do.

Chapter 34

Fiona and Dad sit in silence at the dinner table, eating ice cream, as I grumble under my breath. It's a wonder I haven't broken the plate yet by the way I'm clanking my fork into it with every bite I take.

Fiona says, "Dad, can I eat my ice cream in front of the television? I don't want to miss *Prince Not-So-Charming*."

"We wouldn't want her to miss that stupid show."

Dad pins me to the chair with his ticked-off expression. "Watch it with the tone. What's eating you tonight?"

I rest my fork on my plate and prop my elbows on the table, covering my face with my hands. "Sorry. I've had a really bad day."

Dad's expression softens. "You want to explain?"

I shake my head. "It's all whacked." I stand and take my plate to the sink.

"What happened? Did she make the flip like we talked about?"

I snort. "I wish. I made it for her." My bowl clanks on the bottom of the sink.

"Wait a second. Just yesterday, you couldn't keep your hands off of her."

Fiona scrunches up her face. "Ew. Is that what you do when I'm not around?"

"Ew is right." I snarl at Fiona. "It doesn't matter. I found out some things that ticked me off. Things that... I don't want to talk about it. I need to finish my project and present it tomorrow."

When I start to leave, Dad snatches my arm and forces me back into my seat. "Kiddo, you are not leaving until you tell me what's going on."

As embarrassing as it is, I divulge everything that's happened. By the time I get to the color crap, Fiona has climbed into my lap and wrapped her arms around my neck. Dad's stern face turns soft and sad.

"I don't know what to say. But while I think her reasons were like you say, whacked, it sounds like she realized it was wrong to categorize people like that. And not to say, 'I told you so,' I *did* warn you to take it slow with her."

"I know. I just have to get past tomorrow, and we'll go back to being unfriendly neighbors."

A knock on the front door sends Fiona scampering that way. "I'll get it."

When she opens the door, Hamilton stands there, hands in his pockets, head held low. "David, can I come in?"

"As long as the D and the A in my name don't totally disgust you."

"I come in peace."

I motion for him to enter, and when he sits next to me at the table, I see the concern in his eyes. Dad stands and motions for Fiona to come with him. "I'll leave you two alone."

"But I want to stay," Fiona says, digging in her heels.

He shoves her toward her room. "If they need you, I'm sure they'll call for you."

With frustration all over her face, she stomps into her room and slams the door.

Michael chuckles. "Already acting like a teenager."

"Yeah, but at least she's an open book."

Hamilton fidgets with my crumpled-up napkin. "Here's the deal. I should never have said those things. I open my mouth, and stuff flies out. I'm sorry for hiding things from you, but there's a lot that Kenzie and I share that no one else knows, and that was one of those things.

It should have stayed that way. I'm the one you should be mad at, not Kenzie. She's really upset."

I stand and take the rest of the dirty dishes to the sink. "She should be. Does she have even the slightest idea of how many times I have gone over every situation, trying to find the exact cause of why she turned on me? I thought I did something wrong." I let out an evil cackle. "I wanted this so bad, and when she warmed up to me, I thought I was finally forgiven. When all this time, it was her stupid colors telling her not to like me."

Hamilton stands next to me at the sink, and while I wash dishes, he rinses them, leaving them on the rack to dry. "What are you going to do?"

"I am going to present our failed project, get the grade I deserve, and then go back to how it was. She doesn't have to look my way ever again."

He slings the dishtowel over his shoulder. "Stop. Okay? I know you are hurt, and I don't know what that feels like, but I do know my sister. She's devastated. She messed up, and she knows it. If she asked for another chance, would you give it to her?"

"I don't know."

"Why not?"

"Because some people don't deserve a do-over." Except she gave me one, but I didn't do anything wrong in the first place.

He clucks his tongue. "You are just as stubborn as she is. Totally made for each other."

"Shut up." I wipe the counter down for no other reason than to have something to do with my hands. I'd rather punch him, but I don't want to lose my girlfriend and my best friend in the same night. That would royally suck. "There isn't anything left to say. You and I are still friends. Nothing has changed."

He snatches the dishtowel out of my hand. "Everything has changed. Dude, she said the 'L' word."

I freeze, and my heart melts a little. Not much, but there's a crack in it. "Loser?"

He rolls his eyes. "No, that's the word I would have used, but she said L.O.V.E. Love."

I lean against the counter and cross my arms over my chest, chewing on what he told me. "Explain this color system of hers."

Hamilton rifles through our refrigerator for something to drink. "Apparently, it's inherited. She sees letters and numbers in color. My dad tastes words."

"No fricking way."

"Yep. And I did some reading on the subject. Did you know there are lots of famous musicians that see their music in color?"

Recalling every single songwriting session that included exploding colors in my mind, I ask, "What did you say?"

He nods. "Yeah, there is one type of synesthesia where people are able to see musical notes in color. Billy Joel, Brendon Urie, Pharell Williams. But the kicker is Stevie Wonder."

"Huh? He's blind."

He pokes me in the chest. "I know, but he sees colors in his mind when he plays the piano. Isn't that freaking awesome?"

I close my eyes and think of the latest song I wrote and see blues and purples swirl in my mind. Dammit. If she sees things like this too… It's just a part of who she is, how she's wired. Maybe she can't help what she sees.

At least my colors never told me to hate her.

Michael chuckles. "Don't tell me you see colors with notes."

I squeeze my eyes shut. "I think so. I mean, you don't?"

He pats me on the back. "That's exactly what Kenzie said. She thought everyone saw letters in colors. It doesn't excuse her using it as a crutch to box people in or out, but you do have to see where she was coming from."

I scrub my face with my hands. "I have a lot to think about."

He takes me by the shoulders and gives me a playful shake. "You're my best friend. She's also my best friend and all this is very odd for me, but please don't let her stupid antics change how you feel about her. I've watched you look all doe-y eyed at her for years. She knows what she did was wrong." When I don't answer, he adds, "Just think about it, okay?"

I nod. "Get out of here before we start doing bro hugs and crap like that."

"You got it."

I follow him to the door, and right before he leaves, he turns around and scans me up and down. "You know, she might be on to something. The D and the A are ugly."

I draw back my arm to pretend I'm going to punch him, making him cackle as he trots down the steps and back to his house.

Later that night, I go over all of our notes on the project and decide I'm not even going to try for the extra credit points by presenting it aloud. I skim down the rubric to make sure I've hit all the items, and the only thing left to add are closing remarks. I'm not sure how I feel about this project and the outcome, so I take a deep breath and write as honestly as possible.

This project put me with the one person that hates me the most. We were forced to work together, and at times, I thought there was a chance that we could get past our differences. But like many real marriages, some are not meant to be. The experiment was eye-opening in more ways than I prefer to describe. Even though this person isn't "the one" for me, I did come away with some things to keep in the back of my mind for the day when that person does come around. All in all, it was interesting, but I'm glad it's over.

With that, I pack up all the papers for the project into a binder and shove it in my book bag. Like I said in my conclusion, I'm glad this is over. At least, that's what I try to tell myself.

Chapter 35

With the help of Mollie and Michael, I drag a huge display board, two large Rubbermaid containers, and an oversized carrying case into the classroom. I plop down in my desk, hoping no one notices the dark circles under my eyes from lack of sleep and no lack of tears. I don't care. I have two goals in mind today: get an A on our project and win back my guy. Plus, my Miracle Max costume should be enough of a distraction.

David doesn't even look up when I accidentally-on-purpose whack him in the arm with the display board. "Sorry about that." Those words have more meaning than just the physical pain I caused him.

When Tiffany sees my supplies, she rolls her eyes. "Kenzie, you always have to one-up everyone, don't you? And what's up with the costume?"

"Shut up," Michael says, making Tiffany's neck turn a blotchy red. "Jealous much?"

"Pfft. As if."

Eli points to Michael and chuckles. "Why are you wearing gloves?"

Michael shoves his hands under his butt and says, "No reason."

Eli pries Michael's hands from underneath him and snatches off the gloves to reveal red fingernails. The class erupts in laughter as Michael's face turns redder and he glares at me.

He'll think twice before he meddles with me again.

Mr. Carter enters, and when he sees my board, his eyes get big. "Well, I see our last group is prepared to tell us about their situation."

"Nope," David pipes up. "Here's our packet, but I didn't agree to give the presentation. So, if it's all the same to you, I'll sit this one out."

Mr. Carter stares from me to David, then back at me. "I was hoping one group would have something positive to present. Because the rest were pretty meh."

Mollie gasps. "Ours was good."

"Yours was obviously good, but nothing unexpected. I want to see some realizations, something that will stick with you for a long time."

Tiffany cackles and asks, "Like Dylan's funk?"

Mr. Carter shakes his head then waves me to the front of the classroom. "Kenzie, it's all yours."

"Thank you." It takes me a moment to set up and put on the Miracle Max mask.

The class snickers when they see my getup. Mr. Carter says, "Let me guess. Lost a bet."

I nod, and after a few cleansing deep breaths and one small peek toward David, I'm ready to start. He doodles on a piece of paper, not paying me any attention. Maybe it will be better this way.

"Okay, so all of you know, I was paired with David. He was the last person I wanted to be with, but sometimes what we don't want is exactly what we realize we need. Our job was to have a dog bakery." I point to a picture on the display of the shop we checked out across from the dog park. "We combined our business with living space above it to make our situation more affordable and efficient. That was David's idea, by the way. I came up with some recipes for dog treats. And we even had them taste-tested."

I reach into my big bag, and out pops Catarina with a little yip. David's head snaps to attention. "What are you doing with my sister's dog?"

"She gave me permission. Besides, Cat loves our treats." I pull out a biscuit from one of the containers, and she snatches it out of my hand, running to David's feet to devour it. The class gets a giggle out of it as David leans down to scratch her head.

I take the other container and walk to the first row of students. "So you humans don't feel left out, I made some for all of you. Don't worry, Dylan, these don't taste like bacon."

Dylan groans. "Those were horrible."

David pipes in. "Those were not meant for you, so you should be careful what you eat from now on."

Mr. Carter gets a laugh out of that. He motions for me to continue. I point back to my display.

"Now on to my partner." I take a deep breath before I continue. "As many of you know, a long time ago, David and I used to be the best of friends. But something happened that changed everything."

All eyes focus on David. He holds his hands out. "Don't look at me."

"He's right. He didn't do anything. I did." I remove the mask and meet David's gaze. He deserved the truth, and I didn't give it to him. Maybe this will prove to him how sorry I really am. "I have synesthesia."

Harper cringes and says to Tiffany, "Isn't there an antibiotic for that?"

"No, it's nothing contagious. It means my senses overlap, and in my case, I see numbers and letters in color. In David's case, the color combinations in his name were not all that pretty." I point to his name on the display case, which is a combination of muddy browns. "From my own experience, I noticed a pattern early on that ugly names were people that would do me wrong. Pretty-colored names, like Mollie and Michael, were trustworthy and loyal. Without David knowing why, I walked away from a perfectly good friendship and kept it that way until I was forced to work with him this semester."

David slumps back in his desk and stares at the ceiling. He mumbles something to himself then glares at me.

I look around the room, and Mollie nods in encouragement. "Anyway, David and I had the usual disagreements, but all in all, we worked together pretty well, despite his ugly name." I point to the third section of the board that includes pictures of us together doing different exercises for the project, even the one with four handprints on my butt. Eli whistles at that one, causing David to sneer.

Dylan grins and gives me a thumbs-up.

I rock back and forth on my heels and grin. "I guess what I'm trying to say is that opposites sometimes really do attract. As cheesy as this sounds, I've learned that I shouldn't judge a boy's name by its color."

The guys in the room groan, but Mollie grins. "That is so sweet."

Mr. Carter clears his throat. "Okay. Well done. You and David will get the extra credit. And if anyone asks me about the dog, I know nothing. Anyone want to go next?"

While I collect all my things, I catch Michael smiling at me. When our eyes meet, he winks. It's all I can do. I hope it was enough to gain David's forgiveness. I return to my seat, and Michael passes me the container of human snacks. I don't think I could eat anything without throwing up, so I pass it to David in front of me. "Here. Take these home with you."

He holds my gaze, eyebrows pulled inward, and for a moment, I think everything I said made a dent in the situation, but then he blows out a breath and shakes his head. "No thanks."

My heart sinks. I knew it was a long shot, but I hoped he would accept my apology. It doesn't look like I'm going to get off that easy. During the last presentation, I zone out, only focusing on every breath David makes. With one hand, he taps his pencil on the desk, and with the other, he constantly pets Catarina, who sits at his feet. She stares at me as if she knows I have more treats for her. I covertly hand her another, accidentally touching David's fingers along the way.

The bell rings, and I jump with surprise. As students rush out of the room, Mollie gives me the thumbs-up sign. She holds Michael's hand as they meander out of class.

Mr. Carter clears his throat and says, "You need to get that dog out of here before you get me in trouble." He retrieves his papers and exits the room, leaving me and David and, of course, Catarina. David scoops up the dog without saying a word to me.

"I meant every word. But there were things I didn't say. Things not meant for anyone but you."

He snorts. "I need to cut class to get this critter home, thanks to you. See ya."

"David, I'm so sorry. I'm a doofus. Please forgive me. I miss you."

In a slow, methodical way, he turns to me and holds out his hand. Hope springs up in my chest, but then he stares at my hand. "I need my mother's rings back, please."

Tears prickle my eyes. With a shaky hand, I slide them off my hand, drop them into his outstretched palm and close his fingers around them, squeezing them one last time. "You're my favorite color."

Leaving the display board propped up against the wall, I stumble out of the room toward the bathroom. The last thing I need is for the entire school to see me have a meltdown. He hates me. While I had a plausible reason to dislike him, he has very valid examples of why he should never talk to me again. I don't blame him, but it doesn't make it easier to swallow. No matter how ugly I think his letters are, there is nothing uglier than judging someone based on something they cannot control. So, in that respect, I'm uglier than anyone alive. But it doesn't stop the deluge of tears streaming down my face.

He deserves someone better than me, but I'll never find anyone else like him.

Chapter 36

Catarina sits in my lap, licking my face, as I zoom back home to drop her off. Using my sister's dog in our project is low. I certainly did not see that one coming, and two other Shaws have some explaining to do. I'm not even sure how they pulled it off without me knowing, and I'm not sure who to be madder with.

She yips as we pull up to our driveway. She's only been with us for a few weeks, but it's clear she knows her home.

"Come on, critter. Let's get you some water."

With Cat under one arm, I unlock the door with the other. Fi rests on the couch with her head in Dad's lap. When they see me, they bolt off the couch like they got hit by lightning. Fi grabs Catarina.

"What are you doing home from school?" I ask my sister.

"I had a stomachache. Is Cat okay?"

"I think she's thirsty from all the hard work she did in school today."

"I can explain," Dad says.

I head to the kitchen to grab a bottle of water. "Make it fast because I have to get back to school."

He leans against the door frame of the kitchen. "Let me ask you one question. Did it work?"

Staring up at the ceiling, I do my best to figure out the answer. "I don't know, Dad. It's not as simple as saying 'I'm sorry' and it being over."

"Actually, it is." Fiona sits on the floor and pets Catarina as the hairless dog laps up the water. "It is if you love her."

I jerk my head around and glare down at the floor where Fi is sprawled out. "Is that so?"

She nods and points to Dad. "Yep. And Dad says if you love someone, you don't go to sleep mad."

"Who said anything about me loving Kenzie?"

Fiona cocks her head to the side. I swing around to stare at Dad, and all he can do is shrug. "Do you love her?"

They act like that's a simple question. If they had asked me that a month ago, or even a week ago, I would have given them an answer within a nanosecond, but now, I don't know. Now that I know what was keeping her in the enemy zone, it makes my blood boil. But I do care about her. I always have, and I guess if I'm completely honest with myself, I always will. That, coupled with Hamilton's explanation of how her senses work, sparked an even deeper connection. I see colors too. The only difference is that I don't use it to block people that have the potential to hurt me. If I did that, there would be no one left at all.

Dad lets out a heavy sigh and says, "I know you care about Kenzie. You always have. I don't know if it's a forever kind of caring, but it's strong. I see. That doesn't come around every day." He stares at his feet and clears his throat. "Just don't lose a moment. If I had one more minute with your mother... I'd do anything to hear her voice again."

I scratch my face in a feeble attempt to pretend I'm not wiping a tear away. "I know."

Fiona sniffles, and they both stare at me, waiting for an answer. Kenzie lied to me. She made me think it was my fault she hated me when it was always just in her color-filled mind. She let something out of my control make up her mind about me.

Guilt settles in the pit of my stomach because I did the same thing when I left without giving her a chance to explain. She can't control her colors any more than I can. As soon as I close my eyes, I see Kenzie in my mind. I see her when I write every love song. A broad smile takes over my face because I know the answer. "You know what? I do love her."

Fiona rushes me and hugs me around the waist. "What are you waiting for?"

Dad pops me on the back. "I think you know what you need to do."

I peel Fiona off of me and give Catarina one last scratch behind the ears and race to the door. "I don't know what I'm going to do, but I know I need to do it now."

"Good luck," Fiona yells after me as Catarina gives me one last yip.

I can't let one more minute pass before I get over this. It was the dumbest thing she could have ever done, but if I've learned nothing else from my fake-marriage project, it's that Kenzie is full of surprises, and she'll always be there for me. However, I might need a little help from my friends. I may not have done anything to deserve her dislike before, but now, I'm the one that needs to make things right and in a big way.

IT ONLY TAKES ONE ROUND of begging to convince my band members to fake an illness at the same time and meet me in the communications office where the announcements are made. Hovering over our phones to read the music to the song, we do a quick rehearsal before we cram into the sound booth. At least Hamilton had the good sense to pay a person from the audiovisual club to go out with me.

Anne gives us the thumbs-up and turns on the mic. "Good morning, Hillsboro. We left off one important announcement this morning. I'm going to turn it over to the lead singer of Nash Trash."

She points at me, and I stare around at my friends, who are elbow to elbow with me in this tiny soundproof booth, waiting for me to either make a fool of myself or confess my undying love, or maybe both.

"Uh, I wanted to say thanks for all those that came out to support us at Pizza Perfect on Tuesday. And I want to say one thing to our biggest fan, Kenzie, otherwise known as Miracle Max. I forgive you. This song is for you. It's an oldie but a goody from Fred Astaire."

We begin, and I'm not sure if anyone in the school will understand the meaning, especially when I get to the lyrics about "I used to be color blind, but I met you and now I find." My face hurts when I sing the part about "it's not a storm cloud, but a rainbow, and you brought the colors out." Michael rolls his eyes, but I know he gets it.

When we end the song, there is complete silence in the booth.

"That's all, so..."

Anne turns off our mics and claps. "That was adorable. I bet she's about to have a fit to get to you. Now, guys, if you leave one thing in that booth, I will never let you use it again."

Dylan laughs. "Aww, come on... You know you want to help me record some tunes in here."

A blush creeps over her face. "Music first—"

Dylan finishes her quote. "Lyrics are secondary."

We all groan, but inside I think it is kind of cute that he's found someone who is as into Nirvana as he is, even if I disagree with his quote. Lyrics are everything.

While I pack my gear, the door to the communications office slams open. I snap my head up to find Kenzie standing there, all out of breath. My heart pounds in my ears, and I shake my head to make sure I'm not seeing things. I'm looking at an angel, my very own aggravating, adorable angel.

Michael nudges me with his shoulder. "Good luck, bro. You did the right thing."

"I hope so."

He gives his sister a playful shove before leaving us alone in the office.

"Hey," I say, rocking back on my heels and stuffing my hands in my jean pockets.

She takes a step forward. "I liked your song."

My eyebrows rise. "Really? It was very old. My dad told me about it."

One more step and she's right in front of me. "It was perfect. Do you really forgive me? Please forgive me."

"Forgive? I don't know. You did treat me like Count Rugen for a lot of years. For no good reason, I might add."

She touches my hand and shakes her head. "You don't have six fingers on your right hand, so maybe more like the Dread Pirate Roberts?"

I roll my eyes. "I still think you're a doofus."

She lets out a snorty giggle. "That won't change."

"The presentation was awesome. The costume. Totally cute. But what you said about opposites attract? I feel that way too."

Kenzie sucks in a breath. "You do?"

"Yes, but it turns out we aren't as opposite as you think."

She cocks her head to the side in confusion.

"I see colors in my music." I close the last of the distance between us and put my hands on her hips. "And you're my favorite color too."

Her hands rest on my chest, and I'm sure she can feel my heart pounding a hundred beats per minute.

I lean down and kiss her, squeezing her body against mine. And in that instant, sparks of gold and rose shoot through my mind. We jerk back from each other.

She swallows. "Did you see…"

I nod. "I sure did."

She flings her arms around my neck and squeezes the life out of me. I'm done wasting time being away from this colorful girl. Together, we could write beautiful music.

Chapter 37

One Month Later

David gives my waist a squeeze as we wait for his email messages to load. He stands behind me, and his breath tickles my ear. Fiona has her fingers and arms crossed, while his dad paces in front of the refrigerator.

The past month has been pure bliss. David has written so many songs, and he likes to explain what color he sees when he writes them. I try to explain my color combinations, and he quite often will ask me if names are pretty or ugly. The day we walked past Tiffany, I thought he was going to trip over his shoes when I whispered that her name was as ugly as Miracle Max. For once, he had to agree with me.

David got the email about the scholarship but wanted us all there when he opened it. Along with his father and Fiona, the entire band crowds around David as his hands hover over the keyboard of his laptop.

He squeezes Fiona's shoulders and says, "Fi, do you want to open it?"

"Yes!"

Mr. Shaw stops his pacing. "But whatever you do, don't delete it."

She rolls her eyes. "I won't, Dad."

Michael holds up a finger and says, "Technically, it wouldn't be deleted. It goes into the recycling bin and—"

"Dude?" David lifts his eyebrows and shakes his head.

Michael blushes then nods. "My bad. Carry on."

Fiona uses her cute pointer finger with the chipped pink nail polish to click on the mousepad and opens the email.

David reads aloud the message.

"On behalf of Bellevue University's School of Music and Music Business, you are the recipient of the Henry Williams Scholarship. Through your hard work and determination, you have demonstrated you are a student this institution wants to recognize. This scholarship is a four-year award and will be available to you for tuition, room and board, fees, and books. Congratulations, and we wish you success throughout your college career."

Mr. Shaw stumbles back against the refrigerator. His face is ghostly white. "Did that say everything is included?"

David's huge grin says it all. "Yep."

Michael slaps David on the back while Dylan and Rhett knuckle bump him.

"Way to go, dude."

"Happy for you, bro."

David's wide grin is going to make his face hurt for a week. He turns to me and plants a big kiss on my cheek. "I could not have done it without you."

"Are you kidding me? This is all you. The only thing I did was package it so the committee could see everything you had to offer."

Fiona jumps on his back, and he swings her around. Her giggles fill the air. Mr. Shaw wipes a tear from his eye and says, "I'm so proud of you. Your mother would be too."

He gives David a big back slap then turns to me. "Kenzie, don't you have something to share?"

This is something I've kept to myself until a few minutes ago. I let Mr. Shaw know I may or may not have an announcement myself. It all depended on David's news. Not even Michael knows. He thinks I'm going to the University of Tennessee at Knoxville with him, but boy is he ever wrong.

Out of my back pocket, I retrieve a copy of the email I received yesterday. I hand it to David to read. "Surprise."

He reads the letter, and when he realizes where it's from, his eyes grow big. "You're going to Bellevue too?"

"Yep. They have a top-notch marketing program. So you're kind of stuck with me for a few more years."

He picks me up and swings me around. "Oh, man. This is awesome. But the *B* in Bellevue is an ugly orange-brown and—"

My mouth kissing his stops him from finishing his sentence. I don't care if Bellevue isn't the prettiest word. I'll be there with David, the best guy I could have by my side, and his name is beautiful.

Acknowledgments

To Lynn McNamee, Erica Lucke Dean, and Amanda Kruse from Red Adept Publishing. I am honored to be a part of this amazing press.

To my bestie writing friends: Jymie, Kelly Ann, Mary, and Casie. I love having all of you in my corner.

To all the synesthetes, especially Maddie Dorminy, Billie Eilish, Billy Joel, Vincent Van Gogh, and Stevie Wonder.

To Mark, Maddie, and Jethro. I have the best family in the world.

About the Author

After several decades of writing medical research documents, Cindy Dorminy decided to switch gears and become an author. She wanted to write stories where the chances of happy endings are 100% and the side effects include satisfied sighs, permanent smiles, and a chuckle or two.

Cindy was born in Texas and raised in Georgia. She enjoys gardening, reading, and bodybuilding. She can often be overheard quoting lines from her favorite movies. But her favorite pastime is spending time with Mark, her bass-playing husband, and Maddie Rose, the coolest girl on the planet. She also loves her fur child, Daisy Mae. She currently resides in Nashville, TN, where live music can be heard everywhere, even at the grocery store.

Read more at www.cindydwrites.com.

About the Publisher

Dear Reader,

We hope you enjoyed this book. Please consider leaving a review on your favorite book site.

Visit https://RedAdeptPublishing.com to see our entire catalogue.

Check out our app for short stories, articles, and interviews. You'll also be notified of future releases and special sales.